The Lantern Bearers

The Lantern Bearers

A Novel

Ronald Frame

COUNTERPOINT
WASHINGTON, D.C.
 A CORNELIA AND MICHAEL BESSIE BOOK

First published in 1999 by Gerald Duckworth & Co. Ltd.

First U.S. edition published in 2001 by Counterpoint

Library of Congress Cataloging-in-Publication Data

Frame, Ronald.
    The lantern bearers : a novel / Ronald Frame.
      p. cm.
    "A Cornelia and Michael Bessie book."
    ISBN 1-58243-155-8 (alk. paper)
    1. Solway Firth Region (England and Scotland)—Fiction. 2. Autobiographical memory—Fiction. 3. Teenage boys—Fiction. 4. Biographers—Fiction. 5. Composers—Fiction. 6. Scotland—Fiction. 7. Singers—Fiction. 8. Revenge—Fiction. I. Title.

PR6056.R262 L36 2001
823'.914—dc21   2001028897

Jacket design by Wesley B. Tanner / Passim Editions

 A CORNELIA AND MICHAEL BESSIE BOOK

COUNTERPOINT
P.O. Box 65793
Washington, D.C. 20035-5793

Counterpoint is a member of the Perseus Books Group

10 9 8 7 6 5 4 3 2 1

Sing me a song of a lad that is gone,
Say, could that lad be I?

Robert Louis Stevenson
Songs of Travel

Acknowledgements

Graham Johnson's essay 'Voice and Piano' (1984)
provided eloquent instruction in the
art of song composition.

The Brahms lyrics in Chapter 15 were published by
EMI Records Ltd.

Faber & Faber Ltd kindly gave permission to use two lines
from their edition of John Berryman's *The Dream Songs*.

BBC Radio 4 has broadcast a dramatised
version of *The Lantern Bearers*. A screenplay
is in development with Scottish Screen
and St Pancras Films.

Part One

1

It begins, in a cool glassy minimalist restaurant in Kensington, the year before last.

I'm here at the publisher's invitation. We're talking about a Scottish composer who died, much too young, in 1963.

They would like me to write a new biography.

'We go into the new millennium with this. Something that's going to stand for twenty years.'

It's a pricey menu, so they must think I and the subject justify this hefty initial outlay.

'The story of the man as well as his music. An honest account. Provocative, if need be.'

I nod my head. I know what I'm being asked for. They've suggested a very tidy sum for my labours, which will keep me comfortable in Italy for the next few years of the next century.

Why should I have any reservations?

'We'd like a final decision in the next two or three weeks. As you say, once you've assessed how much work it'll involve. What's available, and what's to be tracked down, and so forth.'

We shake hands on it, Gilmour and I. It's not quite a promise. But the publishers will despatch a second letter to my agent, pretending that their revised terms are a little more favourable and not drawing attention to several new lines of small print.

I walk off, the first stage of the journey back to N10, where I'm being put up. My scruples return, they start to nag away at me: a headful of snapping pincers that won't let go of me.

There's something else that has to be done while I'm in London.

I've been recommended to an intestinal specialist by my doctor in Rome.

I've made an appointment for the day before the day I fly back.

★

At least, I sit thinking, at least I would have tried to script this scene a little better.

It's happening to someone else, to another man.

He's being told that he has spreading, inoperable cancer. In a hushed room a north light falls through taut netting. (Grey upholstery, a toning grey semi-abstract painting behind the consultant's desk.)

And of course I hear myself ask, Are you *quite* sure? Couldn't it be ...? (A case of misdiagnosed symptoms, but I wouldn't be paying top rates if that was likely.)

The traffic outside in Harley Street is just a murmur. The breath in my chest, the blood inside my head, are making a terrified din in the room's triple-glazed, pile-carpeted silence.

The specialist has to pretend that it isn't the end of the world, and not to be unsympathetic. Perched on the edge of the desk, with hands clasped, he has to be a rock: a rock of assurance, and inevitability.

He switches off the display screens with their gruesome evidence.

It's afterwards, walking downstairs around the polished cage of the liftshaft, that I can't hold any more inside and tears well up. I can't see to go on.

I take a couple of minutes to pull myself together.

Outside people walk past entirely unconcerned. Some are laughing. Some carry boutique carrier-bags.

I find a café at the end of the street. In the Gents' I wash my face; I stare into the mirror, I've aged years in the afternoon.

I order a coffee, but I don't remember to sip at it until it's cold.

The pedestrians keep passing by. I hover over them, a pale reflection in the window's plate glass. I'm nearly rotted through, that's what the alternation of pain and deadness inside myself for the past eighteen months has meant. Inside I'm a map of disease and corruption, an obscene cadaver. It's not pitiful, I'm ashamed to still be alive, I disgust myself.

I've been lent a car, so I don't need to go back to Muswell Hill, I can just drive.

Round and round.

One street after another, and I don't know any of them.

I'm still trying to take it in, trying not to be overwhelmed by panic and grief. I'm driving on automatic pilot.

I do see a sign up to the heath. *'Keep Right'*. I keep right.

When I reach the top of the hill, I park. In the driving mirror I look like shit: as if I've had all the blood drained out of me.

I get out. I'm shaking on my legs. My body's cold all over, but my head's hotter than ever, at furnace heat; I've got a dry mouth, my tongue lies on the bottom like a lizard in boiling sand. I have to will myself to move anywhere.

A youth watches me from the metal bollards at the entrance to the park. He's leaning back on one, it's ramming up his arse. Tempting, but I'm spoken for, thanks. And in the circumstances –

He seems to be about to follow, but he's distracted by a rival I have. It's a game I haven't played for several years. I've got a home now, and even if it's far away in Rome there's someone I want to keep faithful to.

But what's the point of faithfulness, knowing what I've learned this afternoon.

I just want fresh air to breathe. I gulp it down.

I walk and walk. I don't notice the human traffic. There's a house with blue walls, in a dark garden; I hear peals blown from a church tower, the quarter hour.

Several quarter hours.

'I give good blow-jobs.'

I turn round. He's young, Latin-looking, haven't I seen – ? The way in, of course, by the gates. Striding the bollard.

'Thanks. I'm okay.'

He doesn't persist, he just shrugs, then melts away.

It's a rejection, but at least I've shown him a little respect.

Something – of a negative sort – achieved, as daylight starts to dim at last. A dampness is coming up off the grass.

It's time to leave. And then I realise that there will be only a few hundred afternoons to experience daylight fading like this. Later I'll have to watch from a window, and after that I'll only glimpse it from the disgrace of a hospital bed.

My heart is banging against my ribs in sheer terror. I'm sick on to the grass, there's a vomit trail down one trouser leg. My hot head's spinning. I get my focus back, on – what is it? – a crumpled used condom.

Unless those weren't my X-rays?

It's like having woken up in a bad three-turkeys made-for-TV movie.

Cut to:

Man driving car.

Cut to:

Traffic lights on amber. Car goes through on red.

Cut to:

View of car driving off at speed.

Flashback:

Backlit X-rays.

Cut to:

Driver's hands sweatily clutching the steering wheel.

Cut to:

Driver's frightened eyes in the windscreen mirror watching himself.

★

On the plane back to Rome I read through the publishers' fax. The words are delivered not in Gilmour's voice, but the specialist's. His is the only voice I can now hear.

'I hope these latest terms can tempt ...'

In an article in the flight magazine, ... *after all, life is short!* The consultant's voice says it for me.

Why should I have supposed I'd get away with a longer life? I couldn't have hit upon a more poetic act of justice if I'd tried to.

From Italy I rang Gilmour back.

I said, yes. Yes, I'd do it, I'd write the book.

'I always knew you would!'

No. No, he couldn't have known that. At the outset I'd been ready not to agree, that had been my instinct. It was the X-rays, not the money, that had tipped the scales for me.

Everything now had a ferocious energy. I had to set the record straight, I had to unblock my memory, I had to make my atonement.

Two ghosts from long ago had to be laid to rest.

Part Two

2

All the way back to 1962.

Suddenly, around the last bend of track, there it was.
Auchendrennan.

I pulled down the window and stuck my head out. Smoke from the engine streaked past, grey like the town itself.

A town lying low on its hillside, and notwithstanding the estuary on its other side a town somehow turned privately in upon itself, a sleeping dog of a place with head touching tail.

*

My parents had sent me off on the train without an explanation, as if we always did this, just like the toffs.

Every summer, for as long as I could remember, we had gone on holiday together, the three of us. The holiday would last a fortnight, the last two weeks in July, for the duration of the Glasgow Fair. Then I would spend August at home, hating the way the days were consumed in that final downhill rush towards the start of another school year. That was the custom.

All I was told was that we were doing things differently this year. I would discover a new part of the world, Galloway, the Solway (Firth) …

I wasn't informed that Aunt Nessie had *wanted* to have a fourteen year old whom she'd met only twice before to stay under her roof, and the oversight – if it was – put me on my guard.

'Hello, Neil.'
'Hello, Aunt Nessie.'
Aunt Nessie was really my great-aunt, my mother's aunt, but not quite a great-aunt's age. Having retired early from her book-keeper's job, she fitted somewhere between the generation of my parents and their parents.

She leaned forward, proffering her cheek to be kissed. I slightly mis-

15

judged my reach, but the kiss was delivered. For several seconds my lips tasted of great swirling tea-rose blossoms.

My 'aunt' had a puffy, plump-ish appearance. Not so healthy, as I might have supposed for someone who lived by the sea, but as I was to find out soon enough she was rather too fond of stodgy food and took as little exercise as possible, preferring the shops to 'deliver'. (She would give her small orders over the telephone in a posher accent reserved for that purpose.)

I watched her as she watched the broad-set taxi-driver load my suitcase into the boot. She had stouter legs and thicker ankles than my mother, but seemed more curvaceous about the hips and bosom. She wore two separate flowery prints on her blouse and her skirt; my mother – who liked to think she had an eye – would have regarded that as unwise ('Chintz is for upholstery') as she would have done the strapped cream-coloured shoes.

Aunt Nessie had a sweet face; kindly but with shrewd eyes, the irises an unusual brassy colour; small white teeth with a gold filling on the top row.

We seated ourselves in the back of the car.

'Welcome to Auchendrennan, Neil.'

Her voice, like my other impressions, was very agreeable.

'This'll be nice, won't it? Having yourself a change from Glasgow with your auntie.'

I nodded.

'And now ...'

I caught a cryptic smile being exchanged in the windscreen mirror between Aunt Nessie and the driver.

'... we'll take the scenic route home, Mr Dunnachie, if you please.'

I had a job to get my bearings.

The narrow winding streets of the old town looked much alike, and one would criss-cross with another. I caught glimpses down alleyways of fishing boats riding high in the harbour. There were broader streets further out, of later vintage, mid-Victorian, with trees growing up out of the pavements. These were the airy houses where the artists used to live when Auchendrennan was discovered by them, where some still lived.

'Quite a community they were. The Colourists, have you heard of them?'

'At what time?' I asked.

'What's that – ?'

'Which period?'

16

'Och. A long time ago.'

I felt that if I were to ask any more questions, the answers would be similarly approximate.

The driver turned his head and spoke over his shoulder to my aunt.

'What about the Deil's Lair, Miss Smeaton?'

Aunt Nessie replied with a nod.

'Aye.' She corrected herself. 'Yes. Yes, let's show Neil.'

We came to a hillier quarter of the town, turn-of-the-century and residential. The driver stopped, to allow us to consider the view. Aunt Nessie wound down her window. I dutifully bent forward to see.

The bay extended in a haze of blue, and became the sky. The sands lay flat for miles.

I turned to look down at the town. From up here it was like one of the elaborate models constructed in the Glasgow railway stations at Christmastime, where you had a sweeping bird's eye panorama of miniaturised streets and buildings.

The buildings of Auchendrennan were every shade of grey. Except for one, defiantly white, a sea-front house in a walled garden.

'So, Neil. What do you think?'

I was still watching the house. A tiny figure was climbing the steps from the shore to the gate in the wall.

'Are you impressed?'

'Yes.'

'Of course you have to be very careful. And never be tempted.'

'What – ?' It was my turn to correct myself. 'I beg your pardon?'

'By the Lair.'

'What's that?'

'The quicksands, the sinking sands. It's an old Scots word for quicksand, "lair".'

She nodded out, down to where some red flags staked out the dangerous spots.

I looked back to the white house. The gate was closed. The minuscule figure was crossing the garden. No, two minuscule figures.–

'What is it, Neil?'

Aunt Nessie tapped the glass of my window, her rouged cheeks almost grazing against mine.

'The big house? Yon's "Slezer's Wark". Funny name, from centuries ago. It's Euan Bone's place.'

17

'The composer, Aunt Nessie? Euan Bone lives there?'

I leaned further round, craning my neck to see better.

'Well – ' There was a little intake of breath. ' – he and that cellist fellow.'

'Cushy set-up that one,' the driver said.

'There's a lot of tittle-tattle,' Aunt Nessie remarked in a more peremptory tone, which had the intended effect of warning the driver away from the subject.

Then she lowered her voice slightly.

'I can't listen to his music myself – '

'We've sung his things at school,' I told her. 'In the choir.'

'Slezer's Wark,' Aunt Nessie said, sounding just a little proud about it, 'is quite one of the sights now.'

Upper Craigs was at one end of Auchendrennan. After that the road wound downhill.

And there on one side of us was the sea.

'Just for a mile or so,' Aunt Nessie instructed the driver.

A wide expanse of wet shore. Pools and inlets. Motion and counter-motion in the sea, disturbances, the suggestion of undertows.

The sun was shining in a blue sky.

'It looks so innocent, doesn't it?' Aunt Nessie said.

I nodded, even though the sands had a keen glare from the sun.

'But good men have disappeared out there. Into the sands.'

'And women?' I asked.

'People, I meant. God's human creatures.'

Aunt Nessie pointed to a red sign. *'DANGER – KEEP AWAY'*. Then she shivered. An actressy little gesture. When I looked round again, she was smiling, so I didn't know what to believe.

'Home now, James, and don't spare the horses!'

We reached a suburban-like avenue, in what was thought of as the 'modern' quarter of Auchendrennan, which had been built between the Wars. The car stopped outside a grey-pebbledash bungalow.

'Here we are.'

I got out and looked about me while Aunt Nessie paid the driver and indulged in some gossip to make up for her earlier nebbiness about the Bone household.

The external design of the bungalow was a triumph of symmetry. A bay window on either side of a sunburst front door, a tiny dormer window upstairs in the roof like the eye of Cyclops, two thin and over-tall chimney stacks which put me in mind of a gingerbread house. A straight path of trodden gravel leading to the vestibule and front door. A couple of elderly hydrangea bushes growing in the sandy loam, framing the two front steps.

My suitcase was retrieved from the boot. It was swung out by those strong shoulders of Mr Dunnachie's which magnetised my aunt's attention.

The name Skerryvore was painted on the latch gate in faded letters. I pushed on the topmost spar of flaking wood. As I did so, the gate parted company from the upper hinge on the rickety post.

'Och, it's aye doing that, son.'

My aunt's accent wavered, in sympathy with the drunken gate.

'Here, I'll have a go. Just give it – ' My aunt knocked against it with her ample hip. ' – a wee dunt.'

I nodded.

'You'll get into the way of it soon enough,' she said.

In the hall there was a coat-stand with a mirror, and opposite it a wall barometer.

Aunt Nessie referred to both as she passed, the mirror and the mercury level.

I noticed on the third wall a Russell Flint print of a voluptuous un-bloused Spanish washerwoman.

I looked into the rooms. They had been furnished from the Austerity range, but the effect of strict moral uprightness was tempered a little by crochetwork cloths and arm-sleeves and velvet cushion-covers made from off-cuts.

Aunt Nessie took me into the bedroom that was to be mine. Its furnishings were more feminine. A lightwood dressing-table, a peach-coloured lamp shade fringed with velvet bobbles, a porcelain figure of a lady in long skirts whose arm had been glued back on. The candlewick bedspread was bright pink, and still showed the fold creases left from its long storage in a cupboard. A sachet of dried, spiced petals hung from the hook behind the door.

'You think you'll be comfortable in here all right?'

Aunt Nessie bent down to open a drawer in the chest, and our bottoms knocked together.

'It's not very spacious, Neil. My *spare* bedroom.'

I needed to visit the bathroom.

I flushed the cistern afterwards, unfastened the snib on the door, and walked out into the hall.

Aunt Nessie was waiting for me, using the pretext of straightening the Russell Flint on the wall.

'Your towel's behind the door, Neil. For washing your hands.'

I nodded, rather too readily, because I was embarrassed.

From my bedroom, with the door left ajar, I watched Aunt Nessie go into the bathroom. She stared into the lavatory bowl for several moments, before lowering the seat and then, on second thoughts, the seat cover also.

When I had unpacked, I went looking for Aunt Nessie. I found her in the sitting-room. She had her back to me. In her hands she was holding a framed photograph I knew – my parents on their wedding day. She studied it, turned it to the light to catch better some quality of their expressions. Then she slipped the photo and frame into a drawer in the cupboard. I waited until she'd closed the drawer before I advertised my presence. I coughed a make-believe frog out of my throat.

'Oh, there you are, Neil. You've made yourself at home, have you?'

I smiled, more wanly than I meant to.

'Now, what d'you say I go and infuse us both a good strong pot of tea.'

In her own domain Agnes Smeaton was back in control of her accent. Polite, and passably genteel.

She left the room. Once I could hear her through in the kitchen, I opened the drawer and stared inside at the photograph. My parents' guileless and optimistic faces stared back up at me, the bride's from under her head-dress and the groom's over a tight starched shirt collar, and neither of them able to foresee the future that lay ahead.

3

Aunt Nessie proved to be as kindly and indulgent as a childless unmarried woman in financially restricted middle-age could be. However, she was insatiably curious, both about my other life at home in Glasgow and about goings-on in her own town. She soon realised I might become a conduit of information on the latter, since I could get out and about and had quickly familiarised myself with the local geography.

She seemed to understand that even though I observed with a stranger's eye I had an aptitude for detail which she mightn't have expected to find in a boy. I obliged, because it was easy enough, and because I felt it went a little way towards justifying my presence in the house. After all, she wasn't used to adolescents, or to offering extended hospitality, and I sympathised with her, and I wanted her to see that I did.

Within forty-eight hours of my arrival the mercury in the barometer had dropped back. The bungalow filled with the sound of rain, falling on to the roof tiles and washing down into the roan pipes. Auchendrennan rain had a tendency to blow inland from the estuary so that it slewed side-on against the glass in the front windows and had to be washed off afterwards with a sponge and chamois.

Aunt Nessie thought she could hear drips on her bedroom ceiling, so – when she very heavily hinted – I volunteered to borrow a neighbour's ladder and duly climbed into the loft to look. The dormer window indicated from the outside that there must be a room upstairs, but it was a simulation. I found no more than grimy bare boards and timber-joists, and the rumbling water-tank.

'Dry as a biscuit, Aunt Nessie,' I said. She looked a little crestfallen at that, as if she preferred the idea of those phantom drips to none at all.

★

This was a flatter landscape than any I had come across before.

The skies were endless, ancient. Water was constantly insinuating itself into the land. Many of the fields – a fearsome green when the sun shone on them – were actually marsh.

The estuary slithered like a silver eel the last few miles to the sea.

Water lapped among the rattling reeds. When you walked close, as close as you dared, birds flew up from just feet away with a terrified creaking of wings. My aunt would refer to individuals who'd gone walking from the town and never returned; sometimes they were folk who had spent all their lives within sight of the sands. Tread carefully, in other words, but even if you did it was no guarantee of coming back in one piece. My aunt assured me, the sea respects no one, whatever their rank or reputation.

On my walks I would stare out to where I knew those sudden treacherous quicksands lay, the Deil's Lair – the Devil's own – but where all that met the eye was beauty and calm.

In Auchendrennan itself, where beauty had lost out to antiquity, my walks turned into runs.

When I reached the High Street, if I was going that way, I would slow to look up at the roof of the Tollbooth and judge in which direction the weather-vane – the silhouette of a galleon in full sail – was pointing. I would dodge into St Kentigern's dank churchyard *en passant*, to read again the prolix inscription on the gravestone of Willie Murison: married seventeen times, and the sire of four children once past his hundredth birthday.

Then came the flesher's, with its grisly window displays. Rolled ox tongues; ox tails; skinned rabbits; pigs' trotters. (Behind the glass a coil of yellow sticky paper had lured several wasps to their slow resisting deaths.)

I would pick up the pace again, break into a jog. On by the Cottage Hospital. Down to the Harbour Square and touch the turret wall of the Customs House.

Uphill again, by Bonnethill Brae, past the old mounting stone and the Stewartry Museum. Up Kirk Wynd, by the belfry, gathering myself some breath. On to Links Causeway.

Watergait. The Boo Backit Brig. The Salutation Inn. Castle Garth, underneath the bleak ruins of the old fort. The Celtic Cross.

Along the weedy vennels, between the high garden walls of the redoubtable burghers' greystone houses in the middle town.

Then on to Upper Craigs, swallowing down mouthfuls of fresh air.

Finally, with a fresh intake of air to my lungs and with my legs wound on elastic, I'd go sprinting on and away from the last of the prying eyes that might be watching from upstairs windows.

I ended up every time on Yett Street, drawn to that peculiar name on the gatepost.

Slezer's Wark.

I saw better from the other side of the street, over the high wall and the dense cover of trees in the garden.

The house was long and narrow and four storeys tall. '1661 AD' was carved on a lintel. The white walls rose sheer to gables stepped with corbie-stanes. One corner bulged out into a round turret. The sashed windows were high on the first floor, and squared on the others below and above. There was a single slim window like a look-out on the turret.

But no one ever appeared at any of the windows. I saw a housekeeper a couple of times; no car went in and out, though, and I didn't hear voices.

I asked Aunt Nessie if I was likely to set eyes on Euan Bone at any time.

'They keep pretty much to themselves. And sometimes they're away.'

'Have you ever met him?'

'I've nodded to him,' Aunt Nessie told me. 'But we haven't been introduced. He has his own circle, you see.'

I nodded at that, as if I was *au fait*.

Bone was being talked about as the next Queen's Hygh Musik Makar in Scotland, even though he was still a young man.

He was best known for his songs. He had also written for chamber groups and for piano paired with different solo instruments. His first opera had been staged in Edinburgh in 1960 – *The Gowk Storm*, about the repressions in a Victorian Scottish manse – and it had been judged the Festival's big success. A more ambitious stage work was in preparation, based on the early nineteenth-century novel *Confessions of a Justified Sinner*, where good and evil struggle for possession of a man's soul.

At school we had sung a couple of his compositions as competition choir pieces. From the mid '50s he was considered a politically correct choice for young Scots voices, following that brief interlude – as it turned out to be – of heightened national consciousness.

The song I was familiar with was his setting of a quarrelling-poem called 'Cokelbie Sow', by one of the Middle Scots 'flyters' circa 1400. The music was dissonant and uncompromisingly awkward to our parents' ears (if it had been playing on the radio, say, my mother would have turned it off), but Bone had written it clearly with young choristers in mind, dividing up the lines into clutches of phrases that were surprisingly straightforward to memorise. It was a new sensation to me, being swept along on those wild currents of sound, where I was one small part of the effect yet also as vital as any other. (Any wrong notes would have been immediately obvious.)

I had heard Bone speaking on the wireless once. A voice with a middle pitch and an educated Glasgow accent of politely lengthened vowels, talking about the rigours of winter on the coast. Occasionally his photograph appeared in *The Scotsman*, the one newspaper my mother liked to have in the house, regarding it as having a more discerning readership.

Bone enjoyed a high critical reputation, although I hadn't thought to pay it a great deal of attention until coming to Auchendrennan. The Scots have a way of cutting other Scots down to size, but Bone was lucky in that respect: or else he had acquired friends in all the right places where judgements are meted out. I started to notice after this that reviewers in the press toed the line of received opinion, namely that Euan Bone was a leading figure in Scotland's musical renaissance. He was praised for his idiosyncratic skills, for what I would come to appreciate myself as the music's wit and its typical unresolved Scottish conflict of intellect and emotion, that timid repressed life of the feelings. Because he was mentioned on the Society pages, I had already inferred – in my coarse, schoolboyish way – that he must mix with smart company.

One of Aunt Nessie's confidantes called his music 'a right stramash'. But loud and bangy as it could be, and not melodious, it had prestige. The town was half-aware of this. I was told their friends came, and musical colleagues, and various hangers-on, bringing a bohemian ambience with them, although when seen closer-to that *élan* might be a bit threadbare and boozy to the nostrils. Any stranger who was spotted walking Yett Street or the Sandhaven and who couldn't be explained was presumed to be one of the 'Slezer's Wark Set', or an aspirant, or a reject. They would be quite recognisable from their city clothes or from their clumsy attempts to be leisured, wearing too unlikely-looking fedoras and cumbersome Inverness capes to set flapping in the gusts.

★

Aunt Nessie had a circle of friends. Jean, Annie, Marjorie, Sadie, Nan, Isa. They ranged over the spectrum of sociability, from the sugar-sweet to vinegar and lemon. I quickly learned how to deal with each of them, how to be the sort of boy each woman wanted me to be.

Woe betide, of course, when they came in threes or fours, but then I lay low, kept my tinder dry.

This was my first summer in long trousers.

'It seems about time,' my mother had said before I left home. 'Since you've got them now for school.'

She said it a little sadly. Perhaps it was because of the extra expense, or because she realised that I was changing. I still had my young voice, but already some boys in my class were in the tenors in choir and shaved once or twice a week.

I'm talking of the early '60s, a separate epoch in the history of sexual development to this one, when we reached those ominous events in our own time, and later rather than sooner.

On my first Sunday I accompanied Aunt Nessie to church.

After the service the minister was waiting for us at the door. He had a thin, aggrieved face. His hand when he claimed mine, only so that we were formally introduced, was hot and clammy. I slipped my hand away again, relieved not to have the contact, and buried it in my trouser pocket.

Aunt Nessie's friends stood waiting for her. They greeted me with an effort at politeness. I was conscious that they were holding back, not conversing as freely as they wanted to. I smiled at them, my coy smile. Aunt Nessie bravely struck up, something about the choice of hymns this morning. Isa and Nan chipped in, all too ready to be critical. Nan had a downturned trout-mouth while Isa seemed to be chewing out the words.

I could hear music from somewhere. I turned round. A different sort of music: modern jazz. It came from a convertible being driven slowly past. A French Facel – I recognised it from my *Observer's Book of Automobiles* – two-toned, white and dark blue. I heard a woman's laughter; silvery laughter – the sort which I supposed people must use at cocktail parties – entwined with the midnight music.

One woman was sitting in the car with three men. She was wearing a pale sleeveless dress, a headsquare knotted under her chin. One of the men was middle-aged and had receding grey hair, the other two were younger.

I only glimpsed them between the departing worshippers. The music trailed behind, and seemed to imprint itself on the air, so that when the car was gone I continued to hear it, those free-flow jazz-cellar phrases.

Aunt Nessie and her friends had fallen silent. They had the advantage over me of knowing who those people were; but I had started to guess.

Which of the two younger men was Euan Bone, I couldn't tell. The older florid man – that must have been Douglas Maitland, the cellist. The woman had been spotted before: she was one of the London group who came and went and never exchanged a word with anyone in the town. The other man might have been a friend of hers, or thereagain …

The car was certainly one of Maitland's.

'One of them?' I repeated.

Douglas Maitland owned several cars. He'd had a large garage built to accommodate them.

'How many?' I asked.

'Four or five, I should think.'

The women shook their heads, but they didn't condemn the vulgarity.

Maitland was wealthy enough to indulge his fancies, they agreed among themselves.

'The cars?' I said.

'Yes,' Nan nodded. (I thought I saw the colour rise on Isa's face.) 'Of course the cars.'

We stood staring out at the road, at the dull matter-of-fact traffic, Fords and Austins and Standard Triumphs. The Facel mightn't have passed by at all – except that the music still jangled there inside my head, as if it was stuck, and I could picture the car and its occupants against the combo riffs from the radio.

26

4

Then fate took a hand.

I wasn't expecting what happened next to happen. And yet I wasn't entirely surprised either. It was like finding something you'd previously dreamed was now present in your waking life; you were recognising as familiar what ought to have been unaccountable.

Even if I'd set out to, I couldn't have devised a more suitable situation for myself.

A friend of one of Aunt Nessie's friends said that Bone was very keen to find a boy with an unbroken voice who could sight-read. He had just finished writing a chorale for boys' voices, and was wanting to embark on a piece for a solo boy's voice. Right away.

Singing was one of my few extra-curricular enthusiasms at school, as Aunt Nessie reminded me.

'*You*'d be as suitable as anyone, Neil.'

I acted out a shrug.

'What about it?'

'I suppose *so*,' I said.

'Don't if you don't want to.'

'No, no,' I replied hurriedly.

I could tell that she thought this was a gift horse with its mouth wide open. And those were exactly my own sentiments.

I tried to conceal my excitement.

'Why not?' I said, feigning – maybe not very well – an air of bored reasonableness.

A woman opened the door of Slezer's Wark, smiling. She was wearing slacks and a sailor's jerkin and wooden beads.

But a few seconds later she had to give way to another woman, older and not smiling, dressed in a housecoat over a tartan skirt.

'This is the housekeeper's job, Miss Langmuir. *You* really don't need to be bothering yourself.'

She turned to look at me.

'Yes, and who are *you*?'

My escort Miss Pettigrew explained. Mrs Faichnie, with a long and unsociable face, hummed and hawed. The swept-up frames of her glasses gave her the look of a wary cat.

Her solution was to allow *me* to enter, but not Miss Pettigrew. My aunt's friend's friend nudged me in the back, to step forward.

The hall had white panelling. A black-and-white tiled floor. A large stone fireplace, with two Chinese porcelain dragons guarding the mantelpiece. A bergère chair on either side of the fireplace.

Mrs Faichnie motioned me to follow her.

'You'd best come through to the music room, I'm thinking.'

The woman in the sailor's jerkin was standing on the staircase. She smiled at me as I walked past, to encourage me. Her smile was a little more hesitant than before.

I was shown into the room and left there. I saw at once that I wasn't alone. A figure was standing in front of the fireplace, with his back to me.

I was more intent on my surroundings, however.

The room had apple-green walls. A long grand piano was placed centre-stage. A cello lay across one of the two leather armchairs.

Music stands. A standard lamp. A grandfather clock. On the mantelpiece, a metronome. A lit fire of logs and aromatic pine cones in the grate.

There were a few watercolours on the walls. And also, I noticed, some framed photographs of two men, separately and together, dressed up to receive awards.

And everywhere, into every last corner, the fresh and brilliant sea light. The room was awash with it.

The figure standing in front of the fireplace turned round. He was stocky and wore a tweed suit and ox-blood brogues.

Douglas Maitland.

He blinked at me for several moments.

A finely featured face that had fleshed out. Receding grey hair. In his fifties.

A silk bow-tie. Gold cufflinks.

I was on the point of speaking, to say who I was, when a voice sounded behind me. I spun round.

'See, Douglas, what fortune has delivered us?'

Euan Bone. In person.

He was at least fifteen years younger than Maitland. He was dressed quite differently. Open-necked shirt, baggy white trousers, sandals and bare feet.

I found my voice.

'Mr Bone – '

He smiled. He made a mock bow, a deep bow from the waist.

I was about to say who I was, but he spoke before I had a chance.

'This young gent has arrived in just the nick of time, I should say. Mistress Pettigrew explained about the voice-tests, did she?'

'Yes, Mr Bone.'

'A few exercises, scales …'

'I shall leave you,' Maitland said, in a clipped accent redolent of gentlemen's clubs and grouse moors. '*Bonne chance*, both of you.'

Bone promptly seated himself at the piano, lifted the lid of the keyboard, all the while watching his companion's departure from the room. The door closed.

'Now, sweet Jesus … this time, please …'

Afterwards he was silent. I suspected the worst.

I endured the silence for as long as I could.

'I'm sorry, Mr Bone.'

He turned and looked at me, surprised.

'You're sorry?'

'Yes.'

'Why?'

'If – if I wasn't good enough.'

He shook his head.

'*Au contraire*. You're exactly how I hear it being sung.'

But he was hesitating again. I looked away, and sensed that his eyes were studying me very closely. Then he brought his hands down on the keyboard lid.

'Excellent!' he said. 'First class! Audition passed, with flying colours!'

I felt my smile of relief breaking across my face.

Bone picked up a book.

'I want to put something to music. An essay by Stevenson. Called "The Lantern Bearers".'

He opened the book.

'About some Victorian boys,' he explained, 'their seaside escapades. Carrying lanterns under their cloaks at night, to recognise one another by.

29

The stories they hear. The fisher-wife who slit her own throat …'

Bone read from his margin notes.

'… and the morose old dame who occupies a house alone with the cold corpse of her last visitor.'

I pulled a face. Bone smiled.

'Never mind – you'll see. I've been waiting to start this for weeks. How soon can you come?'

Aunt Nessie was in her front garden, snicking at dead heads with her secateurs.

When I – gingerly – pushed open the gate, her widower neighbour Mr McLuskie on our left gravitated towards the low yellow privet hedge.

I gave her an account of what had happened.

'Well, well!'

'Can I go, Aunt Nessie?'

'I don't see why not.'

'A couple of hours. Every afternoon. Not the weekends, though. Then we're to have tea and cake.'

My aunt spotted her nosy neighbour, and they acknowledged one another.

'Miss Smeaton – '

'Mr McLuskie – '

But she had other things on her mind than him. When she spoke again, she was only thinking aloud.

'Well, well, Neil. Who would have thought it? Slezer's Wark indeed.'

5

The piece, Bone explained to me, was to be for voice, piano and cello.

He told me *he* would sit at the piano. While I should stand – *there*. At the opposite end of the piano, where he could see me.

'Then you'll have to sing out, won't you? I want to be able to hear all the words.'

He gave me a typed copy of the libretto. There was a music stand I could lay it on.

'But you'll have memorised the phrases by the fifth or sixth time, you won't need it.'

He had worked like this before, I realised. I wasn't the first.

Perhaps he could read what I was thinking written on my face.

'We're starting this together, Neil. There's nothing to beat it for a thrill – for a composer, that is. Hearing the music sung first, and *then* writing it down. That way round.'

Maitland came in on the second afternoon and sank down into one of the squeaky leather armchairs to listen to us. Then he went across to the piano and stood behind Bone, reading the manuscript markings. He asked some questions in the entre'actes when I wasn't singing; he discussed with Bone what would be required of the cello.

Maitland returned to the chair. He didn't sit down, though, preferring to stand as he watched us both, cocking his head to show us he was listening.

Maitland had a softer profile than his friend. Face-on he looked mid to later '50s, and older than the biographical details on his concert pro-grammes claimed him to be. He had been more handsome twenty years ago to judge from the selection of photographs I could see. Vestiges of the young man's self-consciousness were retained in his stagey manner, in what I discovered later was his instinct for a flattering pose or the spots in a room where daylight would serve him least cruelly.

He had broad shoulders, an upright bearing: but – oddly – a weak handshake compared to Bone's. Yet I was convinced by that set-square manner when he stood at Bone's side, as if he was defying the world to do its damnedest.

Maitland only came in that one afternoon.

Otherwise Bone and I had the music room to ourselves. I continued to expect to find Maitland there when I arrived, though; or I thought he would tap on the door before stepping inside in his steel-tipped brogues.

★

Bone had suddenly changed his mind.

He was writing for voice and piano. No cello now. Later he might fill it out with an arrangement: a small strings group – two violins, a cello – and possibly the addition of a solo trumpet. Could I hear it in my head? he asked me.

'The trumpet?'

'That's for the boys.'

Those well brought-up Edinburgh schoolboys of Stevenson's, with their zeal for castles and knights, with their gentle mockery of one another, their misplaced confidence in themselves.

I picked up an unease in the house the next day.

It began with Mrs Faichnie ushering me quickly, at double-speed, through the hall.

A voice from upstairs, Bone's – 'like a bloody little shopgirl' – and then a door being closed.

How had Bone's revised setting of the piece – for four musicians, not a lone cello – struck Maitland?

I began to wonder.

He wasn't waiting in the music room when I got there. No rap came on the door that day or on the following days.

I also noticed that the cello and its case had been taken from the room.

★

Bone reminded me of the children's game where a figure is made up out of mismatching elements: a different person's head and body and legs.

Five foot ten or so. His head was carved solid and square. He had an athletic torso, strong and trim. His legs were short, with stout thighs and much slimmer calves and ankles, but large (size 11?) feet. His hair – a thick mop of it, light brown with fairish streaks – wasn't combed; it would be plastered to his head as if he had just newly been out walking in a gale.

Aunt Nessie would have called him 'not braw', but it was hard to take your eyes from his face. It was fascinating to me, the contradiction between the heavy jaw line and thin, tilted nose and the high cheekbones, the wide mouth, the large violet eyes with their long lashes. The stolid shoulders and slim waist. The large neck and finely constructed hands.

Nothing quite fitted with anything else, and yet his presence must have served as an intense focus in any room he entered.

My eyes would always return to *his*. When he was being attentive, the eyes were outsized ones even for that big face, and at other times sleek and covert. The irises were always intensely that shade of purpley-blue, as if they had tiny electric bulbs lit behind them.

He dressed in light-coloured clothes, which I thought of as continental style.

A cream linen suit when company was expected. When there was just ourselves, white cotton trousers. A white or pale blue open-necked shirt. Suede lace-up shoes for the streets or going off somewhere, and a pair of open sandals for the house and garden.

His movements all had a jerkiness which I felt wasn't quite adult. He seldom kept still. His limbs seemed to be always having to catch up with where he'd got to in his thoughts.

When he was in full verbal flow he talked quickly, and more loudly. He had kept Glasgow in his voice, but it was West End Glasgow – Kelvinside – with its elasticated vowels (the ineradicable closed 'oo' sound) and rolling r's. When he and I were casually conversing, his voice was slower, it dropped back and became quieter, and then I had to lean a little forward to make sure that I heard him – as if I already knew I was wanting to remember every remark and opinion, to sift through in the future.

★

Over tea I learned about the routine of Slezer's Wark.

33

Bone's day started with a cold shower, at six.

I pulled another face at that.

'No, no. It gets the blood pumping, sends it to my head. The ideas come best then. A shave, and then I'm ready to get down to some work straightaway.'

His first creative shift lasted till 8.30, when he had breakfast in the dining-room with Maitland; they opened letters and planned their social engagements. Then straight back to the music room. At 11.15 Mrs Faichnie brought in a small pot of coffee, and the second delivery of mail. Bone worked on for another couple of hours, before joining Maitland for lunch either in the dining-room or on the small terrace outside. Normally he would take the afternoon off, go for a swim or a walk, and come back to his desk and the piano following tea, to copy out the results of the day's labours in a fair hand.

Currently he had several pieces on the stocks, but he needed a set interlude every day specifically for The Lantern Bearers. He had just taken on a commission for a chamber group in Paris. Our project was suffering inasmuch as he wasn't managing to put together a final copy from the reams of try-outs we were getting through in two hours. This might have to be more an ingenious feat of memory than anything. He was trying to distinguish between alternative 'best versions', line by line, and to mark up his choice in red pencil.

Spring and autumn were the times of the year when the pair went off to give recitals. It was the preference of both that Bone should be Maitland's accompanist, but sometimes the demands of composition meant that Maitland had to go off alone.

Even when he was touring Bone would return to Auchendrennan whenever he could, sometimes for no more than a couple of nights between performances.

At other times of the year house-guests would come and go, but they prudently left their host undisturbed if that was his wish.

'What a life, Neil.'

I ventured a reply. 'It's the one you wanted, though, isn't it?'

'The music, I'd say, wanted me.'

'But – ' I ventured the question. ' – you wouldn't have done something else instead?'

'No. You're right. In my mind's eye I've never envisaged it. What else I might be doing.'

'Just this?'

'I didn't foresee I would be living on the Solway either. I couldn't have told you that I'd end up in a house like this one. But that's what's happened. And here we are.'

★

Aunt Nessie was standing in front of the bay-window in her sitting-room, looking out for me. She nodded to indicate that I should please use the side-path this evening.

I let myself in by the back door. I could hear a babble of women's voices. Aunt Nessie, dressed up, put her head round the corner of the kitchen door.

'I've got my canasta folk in, Neil. There's a bridie for you, can you take it cold? I'll have some wee sandwiches left over, and dainties. Just remember to leave the seat cover down on the you-know-what. If you have to go a place. We've got ladies in, mind.'

I nodded, hardly aware of what she was talking about. I sat down at the folding table, placed my elbows on top and laid my head on my arms. My thoughts were still too happily filled with Slezer's Wark.

★

We worked, Bone and I, every weekday afternoon.

I would arrive at two o'clock, and stay until between quarter-past and half-past four. Tea was brought in on the dot of four o'clock, but sometimes Bone forgot hospitality and I either had to go without or receive the tea later from the chilled pot, along with what Aunt Nessie would have called 'the eats'.

Mrs Faichnie knew when to interrupt her employer with the telephone – which was very seldom, and only on the most pressing business. Otherwise our time had to be given over to The Lantern Bearers, to that alone. I knew exactly where the sun would travel to in the course of the afternoon, between which sections of the long wall of green panelling at the back of the room.

35

I was looking at the paintings one day when Bone walked in.

'You approve?' Bone asked me.

' "Approve"? Oh, yes.'

'Do you know about Cadell? Peploe?'

'Are those the artists?'

'I had to learn too. They're my friend's choice. Not mine. I wasn't brought up with good paintings to look at.'

I shook my head.

'I'm not sure how,' he said, 'but I do recognise good taste. So I am reliably informed. Which means I'm not entirely a lost cause.'

He was watching me studying the paintings. I could see him in the glass of the frames.

At future moments like these I would have the same disconcerting sensation that he was recognising in me certain qualities he identified only too well in himself.

★

It was quite natural that Bone should have been drawn for inspiration in his latest undertaking to Stevenson, since both composer and writer shared an instinct for the young boy's perspective on life.

Bone had already set a number of Stevenson's poems to music, including 'The Song of the Road' and 'Underwoods'. Earlier in his career he had written an accompaniment to a stage production of *Treasure Island*.

Although Stevenson had chosen an east coast locale in 'The Lantern Bearers', the vicinity of the Bass Rock, Bone's imagination was engaged by the skilfully evoked setting, a small fishing village tucked between a craggy headland to its right and 'endless links and sand-wreaths' to the left. Here, not unlike Auchendrennan's, was a landscape − or seascape − of coves and inlets and 'sheltered hollows redolent of thyme and southern-wood', a geography of ideal hiding-places for the boys of the prosperous families − of better standing than my own − who came every summer to holiday there. Swimming, fishing, smoking their penny cigars, 'Crusoeing' − lighting a fire of driftwood and cooking apples on it, apples that would disintegrate into sand and smoke and iodine but a luxurious indulgence nevertheless.

The purpose of Stevenson's essay is to celebrate the poetry hidden in everybody's soul. It's precisely this element of resourceful creativeness, the author argues, which sustains us in the dull round of matter-of-fact existence. So-called realistic novels and plays are incomplete and one-sided if they ignore this vital secondary life taking place inside our heads.

Bone was trying to give musical expression to the idea. To show the boys to be, as Stevenson says, 'very cold, spat upon by flurries of rain … drearily surrounded … and their talk silly and indecent'. But they too are capable of romantic, transcendent, even metaphysical speculation. The clue for Stevenson – the poetic expression – is to be found in one particular pastime, where after dark the boys attach lanterns to the cricket belts they wear on their waists. The burning wax lights in their 'toasting tinware' are then concealed beneath buttoned-up overcoats. By their lanterns the boys will know one another; they are bonded in a brotherhood by the shared secret of what they carry under their coats hidden from view.

'To the ear of the stenographer, the talk is merely silly and indecent, but ask the boys themselves, and they are discussing (as it is highly proper they should) the possibilities of existence. To the eye of the observer they are wet and cold and drearily surrounded; but ask themselves, and they are in the heaven of recondite pleasure the ground of which is an ill-smelling lantern.'

The boys' fancies, more used to adventure-story books, are now stirred by the legends of the place passed around. The fisher-wife murderess, who slew her husband and bairns and then slit her own throat; that morose old woman with her long-dead tenant still in the house. Storms, pirates, knights in chain mail, wreckers, men who've abandoned the ways of civilisation and returned to the wild.

★

As well as the paintings there was a large ornate mirror hanging in the music room. The old gilt frame was decorated with faded views of Venice. Misty palazzi, ghostly gondolas, chimeric domes. I was intrigued by it. Bone nodded approvingly at my interest.

'You've been to Venice?' he asked.

'Oh no.'

'Lucky you.'

'Yes?'

'You've still to see it, then.'

'You've been?' I asked.

'Several times.'

'Did you get the mirror there?'

'I think it must've been painted by someone who'd never been. Or who was relying on memory. It's too romantically done.'

I stood considering the matter, and our two reflections.

'Isn't Venice, though – ?' I asked him.

'Isn't it what?'

'Romantic?'

'Oh yes. And it's lots of other things. But the man who did the mirror had a dream of the place.'

Bone came forward and looked closer at the frame.

'Are dreams of places bad?' I asked him.

'Not at all. If I went twenty times to Venice, it would still be a dream place. I suppose if you're born there, it's different. Maybe the natives can't appreciate it. Do you think? Unless they're taken away from it.'

That set me wondering.

'Shouldn't you go on living where you're born?' I asked.

'You have to see other kinds of life. Don't you believe that's so?'

He – Euan Bone – was asking me?

'I haven't really thought about it,' I said.

'Not yet. You will, though.'

How could he tell that? But he seemed to be quite sure, reading my mind for me as I couldn't do.

6

When I arrived the following afternoon, Mrs Faichnie told me they were up in the drawing-room.

I followed her up the staircase. She didn't realise I was behind her until she'd reached the last few stairs.

'What're you … Oh well, stay there till I'm done, will you.'

She had to knock on the door twice. It wasn't quite shut, and I was able to see inside.

Citron-yellow walls. Armchairs and sofas with long-shanked seats, upholstered in pastel pinks and blues. A sofa table, a vase of white arum lilies. A glass chandelier, with crystal drops that were putting a spin on daylight.

A visitor – male, about Douglas Maitland's age – occupied one of the armchairs. I heard him speak.

'I agree. A bitch of the very first order, dear joyless Joy.'

There was laughter at the name.

Bone got up and approached the door.

'End of conversation, I think.'

With an exaggerated gesture he threw the door open.

'I've got someone for you,' Mrs Faichnie said.

'So I see. Gentlemen, here's our hero!'

Bone clasped my shoulder.

'The muse has returned.'

Behind him the visitor spoke, a question directed to Maitland.

'A Friendly?'

Maitland smiled but looked pensive as he did so, a little uncomfortable.

Bone kept his hand on my shoulder and steered me back towards the staircase.

As we passed Mrs Faichnie, she smiled to Bone. Something made me glance back, and I saw that her smile had quickly faded. At a sound she turned her head, to catch sight of Maitland closing the drawing-room door, done in order to afford him and the house-guest their full privacy.

Meanwhile Bone administered his customary good cheer.

'Lay on, Macduff!' He sped us both downstairs. 'No time to lose.'

He strode ahead of me into our work room. He dropped down on to the piano stool.

'Let inspiration strike!' He tucked back his cuffs, then he brought his hands crashing down on to the keys. 'Let clichés abound!'

★

He liked me to see how the music appeared on the page.

'Come and have a look, Neil!'

I would leave the music stand and go and stand beside him. He found it easier to explain when he was standing himself. He drew his head down closer to my level as he pointed with his finger, until I could feel the heat of his breath on the back of my neck.

There on the page were the immobile minims, and the runs of unbenign sextuplets. I got to identify the grace-notes, and the tremolandi which added the haunted spectral atmosphere. The major seconds pulsated in time with the boys' hearts, as their spirits soared or – alternatively – as some frustration or regret put a brake on those high hopes and weighted them back to the ground again.

I drank my tea, looking through a published volume of Bone's songs – the well-known 'Nou Let Us Sing', based on sixteenth-century part-songs.

'The Pleugh Sang'

'Departe, Departe'

'Evin Dead, Behold I Breathe'

'Alace, that Same Sueit Face'

'In Through the Windoes of Myn Ees'

A sort of fear passed through me, at the onus placed on me, not to be found wanting.

★

Aunt Nessie's friend Isa had used the word 'Svengali'. From another friend, Nan, there was a sharp intake of breath. A third friend, Jean, nodded with a knowing backwards tilt of the head: as if to say, we know who's master there, in that house.

Aunt Nessie turned to look at me, and then the others did the same.

I smiled back into their serious faces, as if I could really still be so unworldly.

The Saturday before I left Glasgow my parents had allowed me to take my best friend at school to the La Scala Cinema in Sauchiehall Street.

Dad accompanied us to the doors, then he went off to spend a couple of hours by himself.

The matinée film was *Greyfriars Bobby*, about the wee Skye terrier who's endlessly loyal to his dead master, watching over his grave in Greyfriars Kirkyard in Edinburgh.

During the film I had glimpses of a man, several seats away from me in the same row, opening and closing his trouser fly buttons three or four times. On each occasion a pale object obtruded, like a small spike. His prick. I was too afraid to tell my friend beside me; I would have been ashamed to say that I'd been watching. But I was fascinated as well.

Back home, I experimented. Already I'd felt troubling physical sensations: an initial mass of nervous tension sited in the fork between my legs. Night seepages appeared on my pyjama trousers, like the slime trails of a giant snail and sticky to the touch.

The experiment that evening was fruitless.

I was half-relieved. I felt I'd just got a devil off my back.

'Masturbation'. 'Homosexual'.

There was an association in my mind.

Fly buttons ripping open. A man dressed for Saturday afternoon in a sheepskin car-coat and trailing green cravat.

I knew what Maitland and Bone were, even though I didn't understand all that the condition entailed. What I chiefly realised was that the pair were different, they didn't live by the precepts of ordinary people, but didn't go out of their way to offend them either. They had fashioned their own world, observing their own values, which they protected as something apart but to which they had a perfect right.

★

Bone stood at the window and suggested we might take our tea outside in the garden.

Maitland heard the door open but continued reading his newspaper. He spoke over his shoulder, unaware I was there.

'Cut the lad short in his prime, did you?'

'I've brought Neil to join us, Mr M.'

Maitland swung round. I expected him to be shamefaced, but he was more irritated than embarrassed.

'Yes. I see that now.'

'I thought you might be on your ownsome,' Bone said.

'A likely deduction. And you took pity – ?'

Bone indicated which seat I should take, and sat down next to Maitland.

'Our friend's managed to get himself more coverage.' Maitland passed Bone the newspaper. 'It's pathetic. He'd be better employed trying to write some half-decent bloody music.'

Bone studied the photograph. I recognised the gaunt profile of the present Queen's Hygh Musik Makar.

'The Royals wouldn't know if it was or not,' Bone said.

'Some root-tootin' fanfare. Christ! Haven't they got enough?'

'Might be for some terribly important garden party.'

'Music to lick arses to.'

Bone laughed.

'Bet you wouldn't be laughing if you had to churn it out,' Maitland said.

'You're not taking Maclehose's part now, are you?'

'Only if it means he clings on to life a while longer. Despite the evidence of that godawful photo.'

'Indeed.'

'And if he keeps breathing they won't offer it to you,' Maitland said. 'Like that flunkey told us they would.'

'Darvil? We'll cross that bridge – '

'I think you really would!'

'Would what?' Bone asked.

'Say 'yes', of course.'

'I thought you wanted me to – ?'

Maitland didn't look at me, but he remembered to lower his voice.

'I want you to get all the recognition you deserve, Euan. I want you to put everyone else in their place. That's my reasoning.'

★

42

Bone would tell me that I sang like 'a tousled angel'. An angel – he qualified himself – wouldn't have been quite enough for the task he had in hand for us. I had to sound as if I'd be ready for a bit of boyish rough-and-tumble too.

I nodded at his verdict. It wasn't very clear to me just what he thought, but I was pleased if he was pleased, and it gave me something which I could report to Aunt Nessie in all good conscience, for her to pass on to her friends.

Bone liked to ruffle my hair, to give my shoulders a hearty drubbing when he stood behind me listening, out of pretend irritation: which wasn't how he was when he was truly disappointed by my performance. Walking me to the front door one afternoon he put his arm around my shoulders in one grand sweeping gesture of protectiveness. (I knew Maitland was upstairs and Mrs Faichnie either about her errands or off home, so that there was no chance of anyone seeing.) I was unused to the spectacle of males showing their emotions to other males, and even in Bone's case it was done under cover of a kind of bluff, ironically, with smiles, a purling laugh at the back of his throat, and another clap between the shoulders.

So, an angel with scuffed shoes and a twisted halo was how I would remain for him, most of the time. Occasionally he forgot, when he lost his patience and slammed down the piano lid, when the project seemed to be put in jeopardy. But there were other times when he watched from his stool at the keyboard with his delight evident, with a kind of wonder at me.

" – nets a-drying," I sang, "and fisher-wives scolding – "
I was mystified in turn, and grateful.
" – a smell of fish, a genial smell of seaweed – "
I opened my mouth to let the sounds rise from my throat.
" – whiffs of blowing sand at the street corners – "

Art and creation, and such imponderable abstracts …
On those occasions the process became sublime, and also the easiest and most effortless business in the world. I was the medium of Bone's talent, but I was also starting to realise that I was an inspiration for this music which obsessed him so much, playing my muse's role.

It was my voice he was hearing inside his head.

That was an unnerving responsibility. But I knew I couldn't allow myself to dwell on that aspect too much. Things went best when I merely

43

concentrated on getting the notes right, following with my voice the strange and sunken tunes – echoes of tunes – which Bone conjured from the strings of the piano. I was adjusting at last to the spirited logic of his music, his 'new music' as he called it; just a few weeks ago it would have sounded more like a perplexing riddle of disjointed phrases to me if I'd heard it cold.

" – the wild gean-tree shaken with an ague – "

My ear now recognised severed melodies, ghostly mementoes trying to express themselves amid a welter of doubt and confusion.

" – an ague of east wind, and silvered – "

It struck me, the music resembled the angled planes of reality in a Cubist painting, the sort we'd been taken from school to study in the Kelvingrove Galleries.

" – silvered after gales with salt – "

Sometimes Bone's attention would seem to go veering off, out of the room. He would cross to the window, push his hands into his trouser pockets, and stand and stare outside.

Once he had returned to the piano, or picked up his cup of cooling tea from its saucer, I would oh-so-casually place myself where he had just been.

Out there in the bay, I knew, was the Deil's Lair. But closer to, in the dunes, a gang of boys kicked up sand, chased one another, leaped over one another's backs. They were too far to be heard, so it was like a silent film, played against the immediate sounds of a log splitting in the fire's grate, Bone's cup sliding back into its saucer, a gull passing over the garden. Town boys, the sort I instinctively avoided, with their home-knitted jerseys and holes in the elbows, hoarse voices, distrustful eyes, cropped hair. (From the window I could see the exception, a skull with a bright red quiff.) The decent boys of Auchendrennan had their own gardens to keep to, and friends who fulfilled the social criteria.

Why should Bone have any regard for what that tribe got up to down on the dunes? I gave myself the satisfaction of turning my back on them, disposing of what I couldn't understand with a smile of infinite patience.

★

Aunt Nessie would have my tea ready for me on my return, in the back room.

44

A boiled egg and two slices of white bread, followed by a little fancy cake (a jam sponge Eiffel-tower or an iced fern-cake) and a cup of tea, that followed by an apple or an orange. She knew I liked a speckled brown egg, and also the vividly yellow pineapple fondant cakes in Gavigan's bakehouse window. Those appeared on days when I was especially in favour with her, for the possible disclosures I might reveal.

She would hover about the table while I ate. When I reached the fruit stage, she seemed to feel that her reticence had earned her the right to sit down at last. She would place her elbows upon the table so that her hands could support her jaw. For some reason that helped her to smile more easily, the smile of determined sugariness she used at those times, to start winkling out of me what she could. Her air of meekness signified that she didn't deserve to be resisted. With a cup of strong tea in front of her, she was ready to receive what I would tell.

It didn't occur to her, nor at first to me, that I could intentionally deceive. Sometimes, though, I was a little tired – from singing, or listening to Bone or to any house-guests, or from just being well-behaved – and I found my account a little lethargic and disorganised.

The gas fire was always turned up. It would have hurt my aunt's sense of pride to be thought stingy. I couldn't believe it was done to serve her own comfort, because it grew so sticky and hot in that room after a while that your skin started to prickle. Aunt Nessie's neck would redden, up to her bottom chin, and she would loosen her collar to let in a little air. She chose to sit at the table with her back to the fire, with its orange glow behind her. Gas is a sleepy heat, so my mother maintained, and on long evenings my eyes would start to nip, I'd feel myself filling up with some dense inanimate matter. With sand, perhaps. In the fierce glow the patterned paper on the walls would recede from me; later, with the heat still relentless after a couple of hours, I was crawling up those vine-trellises – past urns and cupolas, peacocks and pagodas – trying my hardest to escape from the place.

7

I could see Slezer's Wark from the harbour wall, or – on the other side of the bay – from the rocks at Vallich Point, or from the height of Upper Craigs.

The lights would go on in the rooms – lamplight – but the panelled shutters remained open and the curtains weren't drawn. As the evening wore on, each window would pattern a fall of light on to the terrace or the garden.

I tried looking through the mounted telescope, but trees in other gardens got in the way. Either I had to satisfy myself with a distant view, or if there was a low tide I could walk across the sand and look up closer-to, running the risk of detection.

Nothing tantalised me more than hearing scraps of sound – voices, laughter – floating down over the sea wall. I waited until I saw water slapping against the first of the rocks before I made tracks back to the town. I returned by the harbour, keeping watch as I always did for the town toughs; turning myself into a shadow, and moving behind a screen of stinking fish boxes and creels.

In the gathering dark the high white walls of Slezer's Wark stood out against the prevailing massed greyness of the rest.

I would be looking so intently that I sometimes lost my bearings. It was as if I was there, in the softly lit rooms, to make a threesome when Bone and Maitland were by themselves, or to be included among their guests. Then my concentration would be disturbed: a box tumbling off the stack, or an old man's whistling, or coarse talk from the nearest of the harbourside pubs.

I would make my get-away, as shadowy as ever, crossing the cobbles slippery with a slop of fish guts and skin, starting the furtive journey back to Aunt Nessie's.

★

Mrs Faichnie was the dragon protecting the lair, defending the men's privacy.

46

Her reward was to be kept on a loose rein. Maitland treated her with great skills of diplomacy.

'I rather think I should like – ' he would begin.

'If you say so, Mr Maitland.'

'But you know best … Just do as you choose, Mrs Faichnie.'

It was a compromise between what he, Maitland, wanted and what she, Mrs Faichnie, was prepared to do. After six years they had come close to getting the measure of one another. There were occasional hiccups, but it was because I was made aware of those that the opposite was proved, how smoothly – just like clockwork – the life of Slezer's Wark ran its course from day to day.

Maitland was the gourmet, with a fondness for lobsters and Normandy pâté foie gras. He had an impractical appetite for whichever fruit was locally out of season. If the best grocers and fishmongers and fruiterers roundabout couldn't oblige, Mrs Faichnie phoned her suppliers in London with the orders.

Bone's tastes were simpler and less sophisticated, much easier to cater for. His preference, even in summer, was for soup and a roast or ham with a complement of vegetables. To Bone food was fuel. That – his culinary naivety – was part and parcel of the man's charm for Maitland.

★

Bone had left his manuscript upstairs.

'I'll just be two ticks. Come with me if you like. You haven't seen the place.'

I was up on my feet at once.

The ceilings upstairs were higher, the accommodation seemed airier.

Bone walked ahead.

'Drawing-room. Well, you've seen into it. And dining-room through there. There's a wee lift contraption for the food, but Mrs Faichnie thinks it's all quite absurd, of course. She's probably right too.'

Double-doors led between the reception rooms. The furnishings were restrained; a colour scheme of pale blues and lemons rather than chintz, and exposed parquet blocks between the Turkish rugs and runners. A formal mahogany table in the dining-room, and a six-legged sideboard and servery. It was the first house where I had seen elaborate arrangements of flowers, sweetening corners of rooms, setting up fragrant currents as you passed through.

I recognised this fine taste for just what it was, although I was quite unused to it. My mother liked glass ornaments, and patterns with busy fabrics, and my father thought that walls existed to be covered over, with framed certificates and horse-brasses and the antique swords and daggers he had spent – 'squandered', as my mother would tell him – good money on over the years, in back-street bric-à-brac shops. In Slezer's Wark, by contrast, there was the minimum of fuss and flourish. While such restrained decor was an eye-opener to me, bizarrely I felt that it was confirming what I seemed to know already.

'*Luxe calme et volupté.*'

'I'm sorry – ?' I said.

'Baudelaire. No, I didn't know it either,' Bone said. 'They didn't teach us that at school.'

He'd gone to a school like mine. An all-boys' day school in Glasgow; fee-paying, but with scholarships which provided (almost) free places for the deserving; endless competition, unrelaxed, and very strong on the Presbyterian work ethic and leather tawse. Nobody went home to *luxe calme et volupté*, so it was considered redundant like the rest of that lunatic poet's decadent output.

★

A little heatwave had started.

In the town haberdashers' and newsagents' put up yellow paper at the windows to prevent their wares curling and fading. On the avenues some of the front doors were left open and a striped hessian curtain unrolled instead. Women got into summer frocks, the men from our neck of the woods opted for sunhats, seersucker jackets, even shorts.

Bone enjoyed the sun, almost as much as Maitland. They had been converted by their jaunts to Italy.

From the music room I would watch Maitland as he positioned his deck-chair out of the shade. The chair would be at its lowest setting, to allow him to stretch out. Shirt sleeves, lighter-weight blue cotton trousers with turn-ups.

The chair would be at a right-angle to the house, which meant he had us in his sights from where he was lying. He might have a book with him, or a music script to work on, but his attention didn't hold for very long.

I saw Bone looking over from the piano every so often, towards the window. If I craned forward and turned my eyes to the right, Maitland appeared in the Venetian mirror, perfectly visible to me in the misty glass.

I'd asked Bone a question as he was putting his papers away.

Did they always agree about where they were going on holiday?

A harmless enquiry, I thought.

Bone didn't say anything in reply. When I looked at him again, his eyes had set very hard.

I understood now, but not as quickly as I should have done, that I had overstepped a defining line. It was the first time I'd presumed to refer to them as a pair.

'A holiday is a holiday,' he said. 'It's not so important where. Just to be somewhere else.'

It wasn't quite an answer. I nodded. I looked away, but I was aware he was watching me, for my reaction.

My eyes travelled round the music room at high speed, careering off objects, and I couldn't have advertised my embarrassment better.

8

The Lantern Bearers took shape.

It was forming itself, as Bone had predicted, round the contours of my own voice. Sometimes I was a little croaky, if I'd run all the way to the house. I thought I might be starting to take a mild version of the summer cold that was going round the town. Bone instructed me that his work depended on my remaining clear-chested. I didn't argue the point with him – about my cold symptoms, for instance – and I did my best to oblige by keeping healthy.

The music had to capture the boys' swaggering confidence and also their sudden terrors. The landscape was to be seen – heard – in all its variety and moods. The tranquil green links; the ripple of water over lug-worm sand; the feisty wind tossing spray on to the rocks and keening through the ruins of the castle, and in a passage of communal reminiscence snatching the crew of a fishing boat to their deaths.

The scoring of Stevenson's words needed to include the sombre and the trivial. The fisherman's widow in blown shawl on the pierhead, 'squalling and battling' against her fate, 'a figure scarcely human, a tragic Maenad', and – at the other extreme – the boys splashing in the sea, disentangling their crossed fishing lines, lying in a sandy windbreak and staring up at the sky, stumbling home after their fruit-picking with stomach ache.

There was no proper narrative. In the essay Stevenson offered poetic prose descriptions. Bone was locating his drama in the continual shifts and contrasts of tone, the counterpointing of moods, veering and tacking over and over again.

I became quite comfortable following Bone about the keyboard, reaching for those curious clutches of notes. He praised my 'perfect pitch', but I had no idea that I possessed such a quality, so I acknowledged the fact with a benign, uncomprehending smile. Bone in turn seemed to enjoy my ignorance on the point. At the same time he had high expectations of my 'sympathy' with the piece, and his patience noticeably sagged if I ever took easy short-cuts, sliding between notes. He wanted my diction to be very precise, even when repeating a phrase for the ninth or tenth time.

'Imagine this is a concert, Neil. Everyone has come to hear you. All those great and famous folk in your audience, just picture them sitting there.'

Mostly, however, I seemed to fulfil his needs. I enjoyed the sense of helping to nourish an idea, of contributing to this process of creation. I continued to experience the same frisson of selflessness, considering myself so much in the thrall of these higher ends.

" – a place seemingly created on purpose – "

The piece was acquiring a momentum, a resolution of its own, a kind of inevitability as it advanced.

" – for the diversion of young gentlemen – "

Vocally we rolled and pitched and dived, towards what conclusion lay ahead.

★

Maitland was waiting for us in the corridor. He looked at his watch: let us see him looking at his watch.

'We over-ran,' Bone explained.

'You're remembering the Napiers' are coming?'

'I didn't, no.'

'At seven,' Maitland told him.

'No harm done.'

'If you say so.'

'What time – ?' Bone looked over at the grandfather clock. 'It's only half-past five.'

'What about the boy?' Maitland asked.

Both pairs of eyes were directed at me.

'It's all right,' I said. 'My Aunt N– '

Maitland nodded towards the door. 'You'd better be running along now.'

As I walked on I heard Bone say something to Maitland about sounding Enid Blyton-ish.

The two men turned away, as if they meant to return to the music room.

I bent down to tie my shoe-lace, or to pretend that's what I was doing.

'First time I've been accused of *that*,' Maitland said.

'There's a first time for everything.'

51

'You should know. *And* a second.'

'What's got into *you* today?' Bone asked.

(I strained to hear more.)

'Nothing.'

'No?' Bone was saying. 'You could've fooled – '

And something else from Maitland, about having been a model of patience so far.

When I was leaving I would pick up something, another memento of the place I knew they wouldn't miss.

A cone which had dropped from the big blue pine. A pebble on the driveway which had an unusual shape or colour and caught my eye. A flower from the back of one of the beds.

Aunt Nessie would continue to question me when I returned home, as eagerly as she had done at the beginning. She would lift the shower-cloth on the table and bring my tea through from the kitchen, with my brown egg wrapped up in a dishtowel. Now she would straightaway sit down opposite, beside the tea pot hidden under its knitted cosy, to hear what I might have to tell her.

What slipped out sometimes caused her to look a little apprehensive, as when I found I was recounting one of our tea-time conversations, or describing what I could glimpse of their private quarters. 'I see, I see,' she would say at those moments, and automatically top up my cup from the pot. She served me so much of the strong tea that my scalp would start to itch. I tried mopping up the liquid in my stomach with more teabread. Bone had warned me against eating too much of the stuff, lifting his shirt – 'Look at *me*, Neil!' – and breathing in, showing me his rib cage corrugated like a washboard.

'Bony by name, bony by build.'

I nodded.

'Plump folk,' he continued, 'have *no* self-discipline, let me tell you.'

Self-discipline, I was aware, was a fancier term for knowing when to hold back. But the bought teabread was always fresh upon the table – a potato scone, a girdle scone, or a muffin – and Aunt Nessie liked to see the plates 'cleaned', as she put it.

'You have to eat up, Neil. You have to let everyone see your auntie's treating you well.'

Stodge and stuffing, Bone called it, unable to buy anything from the local bakers' shops for his choosy city guests, who expected better, which was why Mrs Faichnie had to work in a floury kitchen to satisfy their more sophisticated palates. When I mentioned that to Aunt Nessie, she arched her eyebrows with surprise, maybe with some disapproval too.

'I'm sorry if we're not good enough – '

Her response didn't make full sense to me. If she really thought that, wouldn't she have shown less willingness about sending me to Slezer's Wark in the first place?

I was conscious that many more people than Aunt Nessie's friends knew where I went, and why.

Sometimes the looks were envious, that I should be sampling a grander way of life than I had a right to. Or they seemed to be mocking me, for thinking that what Bone wrote was proper music. Or the expressions might be the censuring sort – that someone so young and inexperienced, a greenhorn to all appearances, should have access to such a questionable set-up.

★

This afternoon I was required to be exhausted in voice, while on the piano chords pulsed and single notes dogged my own. I plodded on in D minor. Several F-sharps started to trail my footsteps, and then suddenly there was a shift into D major. My pace lightened, I was moving more stealthily, I even went up on tip-toe at one point to sing.

Bone had some changes to work on at the piano for another piece, and he asked if I'd mind having tea today in the kitchen before I went. I *did* mind, but anything was preferable to leaving the house before my time was up.

Mrs Faichnie made me a mug of tea, and gave me an oatie biscuit instead of a wedge of fruit cake.

She saw me staring at it.

'Don't you want it?'

'No, it's – fine.'

She adjusted her glasses, those frames which made her look severe and catlike.

I asked if *she* was going on holiday.

'Want me away, do you?'

'Oh no. But it's the summer.'

'If my friend Miss Kinnoull's free. She can stand in for me.'

'Does she need to come? Can't you leave the house?'

'You *do* want me away.'

It was the closest Mrs Faichnie would ever come to making a humorous remark.

'No,' I said. 'I don't really.'

'Well, how d'you think *they*'d manage? And don't tell me, "two grown men".'

I shook my head.

'Mr Maitland was brought up not to lift a finger for himself. He can't help that, of course – but neither can I. Too late to teach an old – ' She gybed quickly.

'And Mr Bone?' I asked.

'*He* couldn't be doing any better.'

She looked over to the door out into the hall, to check that it was closed.

'I dare say he could make a pot of tea. If pushed. And get himself a sandwich maybe. But that's about it. *He* didn't have Mr Maitland's up-bringing, so I don't know what his excuse is.'

'Genius,' I said.

'Eh? Is that what it is?'

'Isn't it?'

'Well, if that's the general body of opinion, who am I …?'

'Don't you like his music?'

'We've all got our own tastes. I dare say it's very clever stuff.'

'It *is*,' I answered her.

'Oh well, then.'

But she didn't look convinced.

'Now I can't stand here any longer giving you the time of day, Master Pritchard. When I've still got the gents' wants to attend to.'

I pushed my chair back.

'I'm not chasing you,' she said. 'Finish your tea.'

Today, I realised, I'd been given my formal entrée by Mrs Faichnie herself, via the sit-down scullery, which was her own private fiefdom in the house.

The friend of Aunt Nessie's I knew as Marjorie was blocking my way past the newsagents'.

'My niece's daughter's about your age. She comes in on a Wednesday. You could come over – '

I stood searching around for an excuse why not.

'Isla's got dolls from all over the world. She could bring some to show you.'

Suddenly I realised what I wasn't interested in doing with my time. Isla and her dolls would bore me to tears. I had a quite different sort of existence now, and I didn't see how I could go back the way, volte-face, to such desperate ordinariness.

I smiled, as charmingly as anyone had perhaps ever smiled at my aunt's friend Marjorie.

'You see, it's finding the time,' I explained. 'With my music. With Mr Bone.'

Marjorie nodded slowly.

'Euan Bone,' I said, adding a little more weight to my reply.

Marjorie took a step back, so that I was free to move on.

'It was just a thought,' she said.

'Very kind of you, I'm sure.'

'You'll let me know if anything changes – ?'

I smiled again. 'If anything changes,' I repeated, and into my voice I put all my scepticism that things would be allowed to alter a jot.

9

'Neil, can you help – ?'

It's a bright gusty washing day. The tablecloth has slipped its moorings and blown across the garden, pursued by Aunt Nessie. The sprigged white cloth is wrapped in the rough embrace of the rowan tree.

We look up at the tree, Aunt Nessie and I, and then at one another, and we start to laugh. I tell her, I'll fetch the cloth down.

I begin to climb the trunk, looking for footholds. Aunt Nessie holds my feet and ankles, to steady me.

I eventually succeed in disentangling the cloth from the branches, taking care not to catch the cotton on the bark. The cloth's adventures have only soiled it.

I hand the cloth to Aunt Nessie. She hangs on to my elbow until I'm back down on the ground.

She inspects the cloth and shakes her head. But she's still smiling.

'What is it they say about a woman's work, Neil?'

I take the cloth back and, for no very good reason, I stand behind her and drape it round her shoulders.

She immediately joins in the fun of these moments. She throws one end of the cloth back with a flourish, as if she's wearing a fur stole. Hands on hips she takes up a tragically noble pose and starts to sing cod-diva soprano notes into the wind, as if she's Maria Callas herself. I accompany her in the musical nonsense, trying to lower my voice.

One of the garden gates nearby rattles shut. We both look towards the road. Where the Rentons' front hedge dips, their next-door neighbour is peering our way. Clearly she is not impressed.

Aunt Nessie recovers her composure. She removes the tablecloth from her shoulders. As she begins to fold it she gives me a conspiratorial glance; she smiles quietly at me, and I smile back at her.

★

Bone had a fondness for the soft pedal, and for half-pedal.

He could play pianissimo for dozens of bars, and that was how he achieved the suffocating atmospheres of the piece: sultry heat, the dreaminess of the boys' afternoons, the romance of the town's legends, the intimacy of the boys huddling among the sand dunes at night, the false tranquillity of the omnipresent sea.

Too much soft pedal, or leaning on either pedal, is anathema to some teachers, and drummed out of their pupils. Bone broke with the musical taboos, to create a magical and entrancing sound world of his own.

I had to go to the cloakroom. When I came back Bone was watching from the window. Something was holding his attention down on the beach.

As he was returning to the piano, I looked out.

The tide was low. Some of the town boys were down on the shore, at their horseplay again. They jumped over one another's backs, rolled on the sand, kicked out with their bare feet or made a grab at their friends, to pull them down.

I could hear them, just. Their cries, their hoarse raggedy laughter – their raw and uncritical lust for life.

★

That night something came out of me in the bath.

I watched in fascination and horror.

Blobby white frog spawn.

Made deep inside me, while I knew nothing about it.

I watched the cloudlet disperse through the hot water.

Then I panicked. Minuscule deposits would cling to the enamel once I'd run the water out, until Aunt Nessie came in before bed. She might run herself a bath or not. If she did, it was just possible that floating in the water would be –

I tugged at the chain to release the plug and jumped up, spilling water on to the linoleum. I lunged for the cloth on the windowsill, and the cake of carbolic soap which Aunt Nessie was using for the purpose. Maybe she had her own misgivings already.

I waited until the water had all drained away, and then I set to with the soaped cloth, scrubbing and scrubbing to kill my seed and leave the enamel spotless, innocent.

When Mrs Faichnie showed me into the music room, Bone and Maitland were standing together out in the garden. The window was open, but I couldn't catch what they were saying.

They started to laugh about something, unaware I was watching. Maitland put his hand on Bone's shoulder, and Bone lightly touched the other man's waist.

The laughter continued. Bone covered his face with his hands in mock embarrassment, he shook his head.

Maitland toppled down into a chair, which precipitated more laughter. Bone placed his hand on top of Maitland's head, he leaned forward. Maitland reached up and touched Bone's wrist, touched his watch-strap too.

The laughter rippled away as both men consulted about the time.

What happened next was over in an instant, I almost missed it. Maitland had just released Bone's wrist and looked up when Bone leaned further forward and placed a kiss on Maitland's brow. Bone immediately straightened up and moved clear of the chair.

For a few seconds, until I turned away so I wouldn't get caught, I watched Maitland watching Bone walk off. I saw the man filled with comfort and pride and awe: the kind of wonder, I know now, that comes quite close to fear, understanding what the loss of this contentment would mean.

I turned away. I busied myself with my jumper, pulling it up over my shoulders and arms. I was folding the sleeves when Bone came into the room. He smiled over at me, prodigal with good humour.

As we worked on through the afternoon I kept returning in my mind to the scene, to the mutual mirth and the two hands reaching out and the contact of Bone's lips with Maitland's raised forehead. Whenever I looked outside, though, there was no one to see; the deck-chairs remained empty, and the laughter and the love seemed somehow ghostly.

★

Bicycle wheels on the road behind me.
'Are you Neil?'

The bike braked. A girl with two pigtails, wearing a short pair of shorts and a Fair Isle jumper, shaded her eyes against the sun.

Was this Isla?

'Are you Neil?' she asked again..

'No. No, I'm not.'

'From Glasgow?'

'No.'

She tipped her head.

' "No"?'

The hint of lisp and little-girl pose didn't correspond with the long bare legs. The Fair Isle jumper was a couple of sizes too small and strained over her breasts. She had sprayed herself with something pungently floral.

'I was sure you must be.'

I shook my head.

She persisted.

'I saw you coming out of those gates.'

The pedal slowly raised one knee and thigh higher.

'That's my business,' I said.

'I'm not being nosey.'

'Sounds like it.'

'Someone described him to me. And I thought – '

'I'm not him.'

She got up on to the saddle. Her tanned thighs squeezed together. She flicked the tip of her very pink tongue between her lips.

On future Wednesdays, I reminded myself, I would go back across the shore.

'He's probably gone,' I said.

'Gone where?'

'Gone where he belongs.'

'Glasgow?'

She didn't understand anything. I stood staring her into the wall behind. She started to look uneasy.

It was the wall of Slezer's Wark, didn't she realise?

That boy she spoke about was a missing person. He was turning into someone else now.

10

One evening, following a phone call to Aunt Nessie, I was allowed to stay on longer.

Maitland seemed surprised, even displeased.

They had company.

'So, *this* is your find, Euan.'

They walked out on to the terrace. Four male guests, and a single woman, Grizel Langmuir, who'd been here that first day. She was wearing a beaded shawl, with a sparkly net on her hair, and wielding a long cigarette holder.

I sat watching them, nursing a glass of ginger wine. One of the two conversations seemed more heated when Maitland interrupted, correcting one guest – a young man with an Australian accent – about Dvořàk's cello output. The young man begged to differ, he told Maitland that he'd recently performed the Romantic Pieces, opus 75.

Maitland was having difficulty smiling.

'So you're an expert?'

'Just a humble cello-scraper,' the guest said.

'False modesty is worse than arrogance.'

'Oh, I don't make any claims for myself.'

'You leave that to others, Mr Quigley?'

'Agents and so on – ?'

'*Not* agents, no.' Maitland sounded sneery.

'It was Euan who told me about you,' another man cut in. 'Very enthusiastic, he sounded.'

'Then I'm very grateful,' Quigley replied. 'That's a fine compliment. Coming from Euan Bone no less.'

Maitland's tired smile faded completely.

Grizel Langmuir noticed.

'I do envy you, Douglas. Having dedications on such wonderful pieces, in your name.'

Maitland wouldn't be deflected. He turned back to their Australian guest.

'You've been giving recitals, I gather?'

'In London. Then Cambridge and – '

'How lucky you could spare us the time. To make your way *here*.'

'I've been back in Glasgow,' Quigley said.

'Doing what?'

'Some teaching. At the Academy.'

'Stepping into Douglas's shoes?' the second man said.

'It's years since I was doing that,' Maitland shot back. 'Seems like a different life.'

'That makes me feel *really* old.' The Australian laughed. 'When you hear your teacher saying that!'

'Hardly your "teacher". They asked me to give some classes. A few. When I had the time, *if* I had the time – '

'Everything connects,' Grizel Langmuir said. 'Isn't it marvellous?'

The others stared at her.

'i'm all for a bit of detachment sometimes,' Maitland said.

Grizel Langmuir laughed, assuming that he was joking. The Australian put on a smile, not to be left out.

'That amuses you?' Maitland asked him.

'I thought you were – '

'That's Miss Langmuir's privilege. To misunderstand me. It's an honour granted by the years, isn't it, Grizel?'

'I see,' Quigley said.

'You'll learn eventually!' Grizel Langmuir told him.

That wasn't what Maitland had been meaning at all. He turned away from them.

'Where the hell's that bottle of Nicholoff? The red vodka, I put it somewhere – '

I had to sing.

We all trooped downstairs into the music room.

Accompanied by Bone I performed up to the occasion.

" – There was nothing to mar your days, if you were a boy summering in that part, but the embarrassment of pleasure – "

Another passage. I aimed my voice into the far-left corner of the room.

" – I recall – with fear and exultation – the coil of equinoctial tempests – trumpeting squalls – scouring flows of rain – "

Our audience listened intently. When we'd finished they all, of one accord, lavished praise on Bone.

The only person who appeared to remember me was the young Australian. He winked over.

Maitland caught the gesture. For some reason he directed his irritation at me.

'You're late out of bed tonight, aren't you?'

I blushed, just like a girl.

Grizel Langmuir glanced across sympathetically.

I put my lyric sheets together.

'I wish I could sing,' Grizel Langmuir said.

'You're a painter. Your powers are creative,' Maitland told her. 'Not interpretative. Singers interpret. Instrumentalists just interpret.'

'*You*'re an artist too, Douglas.'

'Interpreters are replaceable. Creators are not.'

Bone came to show me out. He didn't say anything to congratulate me, but he did put an arm around my shoulders.

'My apologies to your auntie, Neil.'

He took my unemptied glass out of my hand.

'Vile stuff ginger wine, isn't it? Non-alcofrolical, that's the problem.'

I smiled.

He had confined himself to just one glass of Marsala so far. His high spirits were natural, only aided perhaps by the music.

He steered me away from Grizel Langmuir's approaching cigarette smoke.

'Save your voice, my friend. And tomorrow we'll surpass ourselves.'

'*And …?*'

Aunt Nessie wanted me to tell her everything.

'What next?'

Her eyes were shiny with curiosity, maybe with a kind of pride. She kept nodding her head.

But her mouth had a way of pulling back into her cheek on one side which – I only realised long after the event – was giving her away. She wasn't quite as easy or comfortable with the matter as she pretended.

I lay in bed remembering the evening.

The lamplight. The voices, and laughter. The cigarette smoke, vodka fumes. Maitland's prickliness, which he couldn't or wouldn't disguise.

I had been in fine voice. I was glad. It meant I had acquitted myself well.

I had allowed them to hear the music as it had surely come to Bone, in its essential and original state, spirited out of my own mouth.

I thought of Aunt Nessie's pride, and I fell asleep in that happy mood.

11

From the grille in Aunt Nessie's wireless set the pan-loaf accent of the newsreader was dealing out the Scottish news in the usual neat, modest, no-more-than-is-good-for-you measures.

Something about a Royal Navy order lost by a Clydeside yard to an English one.

Yesterday's wrecking of a fishing boat called 'The Marmaid'.

A proposed dual carriageway in Aberdeen.

A visit by Princess Margaret to a maternity hospital in Glasgow.

Discreetly relegated to last in the running-order was an 'incident' in Edinburgh. On the Royal Mile, where a small bomb had exploded inside a post-box.

At the final item Aunt Nessie stopped what she was doing at the kitchen sink to listen. The man's prissy voice reminded us that this was the third such explosion in eight days, following the ones in the Falkirk telephone box and in the parcels yard of Stirling Station.

Aunt Nessie stood staring into the water in the sink, taken out of herself until the last notes of the theme tune had faded.

★

'Lo and behold! Another visitation – '

Maitland himself held open the front door and stood back to let me enter.

' – from the angelic one.'

He bowed, making an accommodating sweep with his arm.

I could smell that he'd been drinking.

'That's what I'm told. You sound like an angel.'

I smiled. I couldn't think how to reply.

'*Not*,' he went on, 'that angels need be all sweetness and light. And beatific whatnot.'

Bone walked out of the music room into the hall.

'What're you saying to the lad?'

'Trying to get him to pronounce on angels. Good or bad. Discuss.'

'All good, so far as I'm concerned.'

'Naturally. But they talk about an angel flying past overhead. Which means something else entirely.'

Bone came forward and stood between us.

'Means,' Maitland continued, 'there'll be a death in the offing. Clarion call, off-stage. *Very* nice.'

'I was talking about his voice.'

'Is that so?'

'Well, Neil, are you ready?'

I didn't have time to speak before Maitland cut in.

'Ready for more beatific whatnot?'

Watched by Maitland, Bone shepherded me away.

'I'll speak to you later, Douglas.'

'When you can spare me the time.'

'I've work to do.'

'And work comes first?'

Bone sighed, pulling the door into the hall closed behind us.

The text today was in nostalgic vein.

We moved between E major and E minor. Bone's accompaniment alternated between staccato repeats with the left hand and sumptuous Schubertian triplets with the right.

Bone explained to me, or tried to explain, what distinguished 'recitative' from 'aria', and 'aria' from 'arioso'. I experimented with my delivery: to tell a story, and then to ease varying degrees of rapture into my voice. Beneath me I heard the gathering force of arpeggios, driving me on, an energy that might have been angelic or devilish, compelling my voice a little higher, and into more intimate disclosures.

★

The weather kept fine.

In the middle of one afternoon session Bone suggested he and I take ourselves off afterwards, to get our heads emptied.

And so began our outings.

Maitland would stand watching as Bone and I set off for the beach or a drive in the maroon Jensen from Maitland's stable.

65

'So, when can I expect you both back?'

'ASAP.'

'Very well.'

'Come if you want, Douglas.'

'What? And be Enid Blyton-ish? You must be joking.'

'Well, *we*'re off.'

'Be good.'

On my excursions with Bone, our 'constitutionals', we took along provisions supplied by Mrs Faichnie. I carried them in my duffel-bag.

A thermos flask of hot water and a jar of Bovril and two mugs. A sandwich round each, with a filling of either silverside or John West salmon. Some biscuits, usually ginger or rice, kept crisp inside a round red tartan petticoat-tails shortbread tin.

'Comptroller of the Victuals', Bone liked to call me, giving it the full archaic ring.

We would go walking past the town and out across the bay at low tide, but never more than half-way between the road and the end of the shoreline, where the sea sucked over the unmarked shifting sands.

'My Aunt Nessie says there are quicksands.'

'The Deil's Lair.'

'Holes in the sand,' I told him. 'You can disappear into them. It's as if the sand is alive.'

If not there, we climbed up on to the rocks, where the spray water had gathered in pools. I took a shrimping net with me, a child's toy really, but it was Bone's choice for us to trawl those fissures to see what swimming or clinging life we could retrieve: spiny starfish, grey sea slugs, hermit crabs, prawns. The smooth shanny fish used a pool as their base, Bone explained to me, making for open sea at high tide and then managing to find their way back: they were predators, like the harmless-looking red beadlet, and like the green snakelock anemones which first lured passing creatures into their waving tentacles and then happily strangled them.

If not the bay or the pools, then we directed ourselves to higher ground, the bracken brakes on the headland, which led – by way of some spectacular views – to Rosmailzie Forest. Three or four times Bone drove us both there.

Aunt Nessie looked puzzled when I tried to describe the forest to her.

'Whyever would he want to take you somewhere like that?'

Then her eyes narrowed, and that occasional expression of disquiet crossed her face: the way in which clouds, from our vantage point on the path beaten through the bracken, would ripple as the briefest shadows over the bay's shiny wet sand.

But her features settled again as she reassured herself, having me here safe and sound in front of her.

'It's years since I've been up yonder,' she said. 'It's just a wood, isn't it?'

'Oh, a very old one,' I explained patiently. 'Medieval.' And, I added, it was supposed to contain more than forty trees.

'It must be an awfully wee forest now. Only forty trees?'

'No, forty types,' I clarified, rather hurriedly.

'Oh. *Types*,' she repeated, and she tried to laugh.

I lowered my eyes to the table cloth and vaguely drew the outline of Rosmailzie Forest with a finger, a clumsy lacy geography not nearly as accurate as the one I recreated in my mind last thing at night, to go wandering back into while I lay in bed after Aunt Nessie's lights-out, in the final moments of bleary consciousness before sleep.

I never went into the old forest alone, though. I didn't have the courage to go by myself. Even in summer, high summer, daylight there was in short supply.

When we reached a clearing Bone and I would stand on the carpet of pine needles and tilt our heads and see sky directly above us; but the further off I looked, in all directions, the darker the place became. Bone brought a torch with him, and we played the beams of light into the distance, as far as the bulb could track. One of us held the torch and the other would make shadow figures. On our first couple of forays I shouted, attempting to throw my voice to the top of the highest tree, until eventually Bone warned me that that sort of thing would do my voice no good, none at all.

After that Bone started giving me vocal exercises to perform on our walks. He wondered aloud about the effects of too much fresh air, but told himself it ought to strengthen my vocal chords.

He would sing a guide note, and I would produce a scale from that, rising and descending, majors and minors, chromatic semi-tones and whole tones, even Scottish pentatonic. He advised me how to let my diaphragm drop and my ribs expand to produce sounds, how to sustain notes by controlling my breath with rapid intakes and long emissions, the difference between head-register and chest-register, the manufacture of falsetto using the raised larynx. From scales we progressed to little phrases, which he would construct for me and which I would repeat. And repeat and repeat, as many times as he asked me to. Phrases were added to phrases, and Bone would remove some folded sheets of paper from his pocket to dash down the notes in elementary staff notation.

He was mostly patient with me, but not always. Now and then I felt I was just a mechanical voice-box, when his friendliness seemed to be forgotten, when he was giving himself to the music and nothing else, and I realised what my aunt's friend Nan McCurtain had meant by saying that *she*'d heard he could strike women as being 'quite charmless' if he wasn't in a mood for humouring mixed company. He hadn't a social demeanour even for me then, but I never lost my sense of innate usefulness and ultimate purpose. When I seemed to be most ignored, I knew that this was only a temporary state of affairs. Indeed afterwards he would be especially indulgent, stashing the loose sheets of paper back into his pocket, joining me at the rock pools, letting me run across the sand or hurl pine cones up into the trees' stratosphere; he would remember rhymes from his childhood, slang he'd used at school, the nicknames which his professors were called at the Academy of Music in Glasgow, the practical jokes he and the other students got up to.

His manner completely lightened then, and he was a different man. He would fasten his hand on my shoulders and draw me close to him, close enough for me to feel the contours of his legs and hips through the material of his trousers. If I mentioned having to return home, he would sigh before speaking of my aunt.

'And what are Miss Smeaton's plans for this evening? Her need of you is greater than mine, I suppose?'

The delivery was sotto voce, indeed affectionate, without the waspishness – put on a little diffidently, amateurishly, to compete with Maitland's – whenever he had an audience and he'd speak of 'your revered Aunt Agnes' or 'the good Hausfrau'.

★

It happened again in the bath.
I knew not to panic this time.

I lay back, closed my eyes, waited for the emission to finish.

Currents of pleasure passed through me, rising then diminishing, from the crown of my head to my feet, to each of my tightly clenched toes.

★

Another small bomb had gone off in a post-office collection box in Glasgow, in the centre of the city.

Maitland stood at the window, with his back to the light, reading the story out of a newspaper to Bone.

' "A young man",' he continued, ' "has been apprehended for questioning by the authorities".'

Momentarily Bone glanced in my direction. He crooked his little finger to remove something from the corner of one eye, and flicked the irritant away.

'What else?' he asked.

Maitland looked over the top of his newspaper.

'What pleasanter news do you have for us, Douglas?'

Maitland was going to speak, but Bone silenced him with a brittle smile.

'We have our young guest to keep amused, don't we? We mustn't forget Neil McNeil of McNeil, must we now?'

At this point, Bone said, we needed a vision of calm in the piece.

Night. The sea was stilled, the boys slept soundly in their beds. The would-be suicide was lying quietly in jail, the madwoman was sitting out the long watch in silence with her dead house-guest.

I listened while Bone played. A delicate shimmer of notes dropped to impeccable cadences.

When I did sing, it was to shift the mood briefly into elegy.

" – School time was drawing near, and the nights were already black – "

My vocal line was held, suspended, over a slow ground-bass. Bone's part and mine hardly seemed to be referring to each other, and yet to achieve that effect the notation had to be worked over again and again and again, so that I understood precisely – as he did – how each note must fall. There could be no room for error.

Afterwards Bone clasped me, he put his arm across both shoulders, opened his hand on the back of my neck. Yet it was a stilted, awkward gesture. I wanted to be held by him, to have his full embrace. Please.

I smiled, only meaning to encourage him, to put him at his ease. My smile seemed to be disconcerting him, however. He withdrew his arm, glanced at his watch.

'I've got to get some things off in the post. Would you mind if I leave you in Mrs Faichnie's capable ...?'

12

At first I thought Aunt Nessie was talking to one of her telephone friends, someone with the same name as my mother. Then it occurred to me that it must be my mother, because the tone was more confidential than Aunt Nessie's usual. I hadn't been summoned to speak, and was eavesdropping from behind the living-room door.

'Husbands,' Aunt Nessie was saying, 'aren't in such plentiful supply, Kay. Take my word for it.'

Breathe in, breathe out.

'Well, I know I can't dissuade you if you've made up your mind.'

She didn't try.

'It is a big step,' she said, with a warning ring in her voice.

As she let my mother talk, she stood turning the fringes of the rug with the toe of her shoe. Every so often she would sigh. If there were any more things she could have said, she was holding them back.

Aunt Nessie shook her head at the rug. She looked up at one point, found her reflection in the pewter-framed mirror on the coat-stand, pulled at a strand of loose hair on one side of her face with two pernickety fingers. Her mouth vaguely pouted, then her lips flexed as if they were meaning to shape themselves around some words. The words weren't spoken, though. Nothing came out, except another sigh; but it was a long and, as sighs go, expressive one, carefully directed into the mouthpiece, so that it should seem on future retrospection by her niece to have been sympathetic and quite blameless.

She rubbed at tiny marks on the table-top with a licked finger. Then she coaxed the flowers in the vase to stand taller. She remembered to stand a little taller herself.

Aunt Nessie didn't mention the phone call. I had to ask about it. She didn't say whom she had been speaking to. 'I was just arranging something,' she told me.

She smiled blearily over my head while her eyes sought the window, crinkling against the sunset light and the usefulness of long distance.

Aunt Nessie had been a book-keeper, first in a firm of auctioneers in the town and then in a lawyers' practice.

I couldn't see her keeping a tally of rams sold and bullocks which had failed to meet their reserve price. But she'd been happier working alongside those bluff stock-men in loud waistcoats and corn-yellow corduroy; or maybe it was because she'd been younger then that she'd received more compliments, from free and easy types who didn't stand on anyone's dignity.

The lawyers' practice, by comparison, had lacked any sense of fun. *But* – Aunt Nessie ventured to admit to me late one evening – they'd had their minds on profitable ruses there, and some of them barely legal, never mind taking on cases (at inflated fees) where the defendant's guilt could be in no doubt but where they'd persuade you black was white.

I had to remind myself that she hadn't always lived like this, as a Hausfrau on Hauselock Avenue. She'd had routines at work, and colleagues, and a private code for confidences, and jealousies, and she'd needed to learn to judge human nature from its concealments and evasions.

★

Maitland was having problems with his back.

The pains were nothing new, but they came and went. They came whenever he was obliged to sleep on a sagging mattress, or had to travel for a long while in the same sitting position, or – as must have been the case now – when he found himself undergoing some mental stress.

Mrs Faichnie recognised the signs, and was discussing them at the kitchen table with Mrs Lorimer, who did the char work Mrs Faichnie thought was beneath her. The two women lifted their eyes from the tea in their cups and stared at me when I walked in. There was silence. Mrs Lorimer's hostile stare hoisted me up on the coat hook behind the door, as if she was demanding a confession from me: so, what do you know, sonny? what have you seen? never mind the beatific whatnot, just spill the beans.

'I'll be going,' I said – and a few seconds later I'd gone.

★

It was the house that had brought Maitland and Bone here.

They had been sent particulars of several properties, in different corners of Scotland, and Slezer's Wark was the one that they were most enthusiastic about. Neither had been to Auchendrennan before, or even knew the Solway. Dumfries thirty miles away connected to the London railway line; they'd be able to drive to Glasgow in just over three hours, less than four to Edinburgh, and they had friends in both cities where they could put up overnight to catch a concert or recital.

Auchendrennan had once been home to fashionable artists, and the scenery and clear light still brought aficionados.

It wasn't the end of the world, by any means.

But would they have opted to settle here if they hadn't happened to arrive in an autumn fog and depart in a sea haar, having seen so little of it?

The greyness and compactness, the locals' combined narrowness and prurience. It all counteracted the appeal of the house, but evidently not enough to change the men's minds about having come.

That weird name. ('Wark' meant a fort or imposing building. It was named after an ambitious local merchant of long ago, one Slezer, who had somehow made a fortune for himself from salt panning and burning seaweed into kelp.)

Maitland and Bone had lasted six years, and endured the rumour-mill.

Home *used* to be in London.

I asked Bone, did they go back often?

'To London? No, not at all.'

'Why not?'

'We live *here*.'

That wasn't an answer, I felt.

'Don't you ever want to go?'

'What's that?'

He must have heard me perfectly well, but I repeated the question anyway. Did he never want to go to London?

'Now and then, yes. But ...'

'When your friends tell you about it?'

'I wouldn't get my work done in London. I can do my work here.'

'Not even for a holiday?'

'Not even for a holiday.'

My disbelief must have been showing on my face.

'Don't you think I work hard?' he asked.

'Yes,' I said. 'Yes. It's just – '

'How kind of you to be concerned about my taking enough rest. But if I wanted a holiday – and we *do* have holidays – '

I noted the change from singular to plural pronoun, and he seemed to hear it too.

' – if my friend and I choose to go somewhere, it'll be a proper holiday place, a resort.'

Their favourite holiday destination was Italy.

Venice. Capri. Como. Bordighera. And their current enthusiasm, Portofino.

I had seen the picturesque waterfront at Portofino on a BEA poster in a Glasgow travel agent's window. And the newspapers had shown the Duke and Duchess of Windsor walking their pugs along the quayside. I could picture Bone and Maitland with the dusty-coloured buildings behind them, sitting at their special table in their regular *ristorante* with its striped awning and window-boxes.

They might have gone to live there after they'd left London.

'That was one possibility,' Bone told me one afternoon out on the terrace, during tea.

'Oh yes. It was definitely on the cards,' Maitland confirmed.

But Scotland had won out.

'If you'd gone to Italy,' I said, 'then you mightn't have written The Lantern Bearers.'

'DV it gets finished all right,' Maitland added quickly, reaching out and touching a piece of wood.

'Well, you wouldn't have been there,' Bone admitted to me. 'No Neil, not in Italy.'

I fished. 'Maybe someone else ...'

'This is all very Scottish,' Maitland said.

'What?' Bone leaned back in the basket chair. 'Talking about Italy is?'

'Talking hypothetically like this. "If – " "If only – " "Could've been", "might've been". The Scots' disease. Am I not right?'

Bone nodded.

'You're always right, Douglas.'

The two men exchanged private glances.

Sometimes, though, I felt these surroundings might almost be incidental to Bone.

When he was fully involved in composing, he was aware of nothing else except the work. Whatever might be in front of his eyes, his mind's eye was seeing only Stevenson's boys: scrambling about the high grassy cliffs, night figures in cloaks wearing lanterns clipped to their belts.

He was too busy some afternoons even to look out of the music room window, too intent to hear the knuckle rap on the door or the query 'Euan? Can I speak to you a moment?' or to note that long expectant silence before Maitland decided to leave well alone this time.

Now the Victorian boys were cockily parading along the harbour wall. The accents in my vocal line fell a crotchet behind the bar-line.

Later, the boys broke into a run, their heart-rate increased, after some small provocation – answering back – done to one of the shopkeepers.

Bone worked at a clever rubato in the quaver triplets of the voiceless section, drawing out the melody I'd been singing just with the little finger of his right hand.

Bone didn't drink much, but Maitland needed no persuading.

His doctor in London had warned him off all alcohol, threatened him with talk of liver cirrhosis. Dr Joss here in Auchendrennan had read the same tell-tale signs, but hadn't spoken so bluntly on the subject. Maitland had persuaded himself there couldn't be so much harm as they were claiming.

I heard Bone saying something to him one day, wasn't it a bit early to be thinking about a snifter?

'I can handle it.'

'You were told you shouldn't.'

'I think I know myself better than Percival or Joss ever will.'

'Well, just remember.'

Remember what?

I heard the top of the gin bottle rattling on the salver, then (after, I supposed, a loud swallow which I couldn't pick up) the tumbler going down on top of the sideboard.

Once, Mrs Faichnie told me, she had found Mr Bone sitting at his work in the summerhouse, soaked to the skin. His chair was positioned close to the open window, and he had quite failed to notice how heavily the rain was falling.

She shook her head, in pitying admiration of intellectual cleverness and its eccentricities.

★

From the hall in the bungalow I heard Aunt Nessie being asked over canasta about her HFs.

Hot Flushes were WPs. Women's Problems.

(Embarrassing terms were habitually contracted in this way.)

'Everyone's in the same boat. Eventually. I can't complain.'

Isa and Marjorie and the others recounted their experiences, and it was a little like a freemasonry of suffering. There was some talk as to whether Aileen Ross had got away more luckily than the rest; until it was suggested that she might have had a false start, and would end up with a double dose, which prospect seemed not to discomfit Aunt Nessie or her friends at all.

★

I listened to the silence from upstairs.

'They're not back yet,' Mrs Faichnie said, closing the front door behind me.

I asked where they were.

'Driven to the station with their pals.'

'Oh.'

'Friends,' she corrected herself.

I was hurried through the hall notwithstanding.

'And I've to be at the dentist's surgery by quarter-past.' She read her watch. 'I'll have to get going.' She undid the buttons of her housecoat. 'If they're not back in five minutes …'

Five minutes later they still weren't back.

She said, she'd need to leave me alone in the house. I was on my honour, mind. Not a thought of mischief, because she'd know at once. She could smell any trouble in the air – so I'd been warned.

I assured her that everything would be okay.

'Speak the Queen's English, please.'

'Everything will be fine,' I said.

'Very well, then. Just this once. I've got a nagging tooth.'

I walked with her to the front door.

'I'll shut the door for you,' I said.

'No misbehaving now. Or it'll be the high jump for you, m'lad.'

I waited until she would have reached the end of the driveway. I listened. There was no sound of car wheels on the gravel. I couldn't hear a powerful engine approaching.

I was up the two flights of stairs to the second floor in thirty seconds flat.

I pushed a door open.

One room led into another beyond. The first, the larger, was a bed-room, furnished with a double bed and a chest of drawers with a mirror on top and a couple of armchairs.

The second room was a dressing-room. A giant double-wardrobe filled almost half of it. A white-faced intruder watched me from one corner, and I saw myself looking small and insignificant in the tilted mirror.

I was in Maitland's quarters. His green loden cape was laid over the back of the armchair, and I recognised as his the pair of suede demi-brogues, with wooden trees dutifully inserted.

A Maitland family portrait hung over the fireplace. Photographs, some framed, were set out on the mantelpiece. Bone featured in most of them, with or without Maitland.

Beside the basin in the corner was a bottle, unopened, filled with tarry black liquid. I lifted it up. The label carried only a name, 'Noirette Pour Hommes', and a line illustration of a man's head with evenly black, slicked back hair; middle-aged as he was, the man in the drawing smiled with the brash confidence of youth.

★

Aunt Nessie held up the two scarves.

'Well ... what d'you think, Neil? With this green dress – and that fawn woolly if it turns chilly.'

I thought lemon preferable to the pink, although neither seemed very apt.

'The yellow one? Yes. I do believe you're right.'

She beamed over at me.

'You've got an eye for colour, I can tell.'

Now and then she would consult me.

These shoes or those ones? This bangle? – or that bracelet? White geraniums by the back door, or red? Floral curtains for the bathroom next, or a geometric pattern?

She waited for me to answer. She considered what I said. Then she would nod, and smile; she would tell me, funny, that was the very same conclusion she'd come to herself.

13

Nietzsche wrote, the perfect artist is for ever shut off from all reality.

Bone may have been more detached than I gave him credit for being. He may not have seen hazards looming, and every life has those. It seemed to be an enchanted life, but Maitland must have known that actuality had to be kept at a distance, for the sake of the music. Bone was preserved from distraction, but he was also left vulnerable to harmful elements. There were critics and snipers and leeches, and Maitland banished as many of those as he could; some of the excluded might have proved less spiteful if Maitland had simply tried to humour them.

As for myself – I was an exception. I'd been admitted, and kept on. They had decided that I was too necessary, and so they were ready to grant me some leeway. At the same time they'd had to lower their guard.

*

"Behold – a posse of silent people escorting a cart, and on the cart, bound in a chair, her throat bandaged, and the bandage was all bloody – horror! – "

It was as if … as if somehow I already knew the music, it was only waiting there inside me. Or rather, the power lay with Bone to charm music out of me, because he knew the magical methods. We conspired together.

" – the fisher-wife herself, who continued to ride my thoughts, and even today (as I recall the scene) darkens daylight – "

Maitland happened to be putting his car in the garage as I walked past. He called me over.

'You *do* understand – that you mustn't discuss your time here. I mean, the work you do here in the music room.'

I was trying to think who I might have told. Apart from Aunt Nessie, that is.

'Yes?' he asked me.

I nodded.

'I'm sure you won't have said. But you'll know that for yourself, won't you? It's something you have an instinct about, I'm sure.'

I didn't like to contradict him. I nodded again.

'I'm depending on you, Neil. The process of work is sacred. It's Mr Bone's superstition. And mine.'

'Yes,' I said.

Maitland permitted himself to smile.

'Then we shan't refer to the matter again.'

★

Going home I would take off my pullover and drape it around my shoulders, as Bone did. It took a lot of care to knot it so casually.

Dressed like that, my walk was different, looser. I was insouciant, like a boulevardier. My arms would swing rhythmically, speeding me along.

But my nerve would fail me as soon as I reached Mrs Mac's house on the corner, on the final straight home. I undid the knot and pulled the jumper off, bundled it under my arm. That popinjay belonged between here and Yett Street, not to Dundas Avenue and Hauselock.

They would be waiting for me, Aunt Nessie's friends, in the front gardens of their bungalows, watering thirsty hydrangeas or snicking the spent rose blooms. I would race past, throwing a terse 'Good evening' over my shoulder. I didn't stop until I reached Skerryvore.

Aunt Nessie would have my tea prepared, and her questions ready too. All the way home I would have been planning just what to tell her and what not. She accepted whatever I offered her, but she had a more highly tuned intelligence for gossip than I was aware of, and invariably more would be extracted from me than I intended should happen.

If she tricked me it was very subtly done. She only had to say a word, half a sentence, and I would suppose I must have mentioned it already, and begin to explain before it occurred to me that … Her smiles seemed quite disingenuous, she would sit fussing with the crockery or the cutlery, so I didn't feel I was quite justified in suspecting her. But her eyes when she raised them were canny and clear.

★

Bone started to take me swimming in the sea, where the bathing would be safe and where there would be fewer people.

He provided me with a towelling wrap, which I put on over my trunks when I changed at Slezer's Wark. It reached to my ankles, but I loved the weight and softness of the fabric. On swimming days we took the car down to the beach, and back again, dripping water on to the Jensen's maroon leather and carpet.

Bone had a way of swimming on his side, so that he was able to look both forwards and behind. He also floated on his back; it appeared easy to do, but for me it wasn't. I required all my concentration just to be able to manage my slapdash breaststroke in the cold currents.

On the drive back afterwards I laid my arm on the walnut window sill and smelt iodine from the sea. Bone would turn and smooth down my hair with his hand, telling me that I should have remembered to dry it myself, but – every time – failing to remind me as we ran out of the sea and up the ramp of sand to the rock where we had left our towelling robes. I forgot, or rather I couldn't be bothered, and so the same ritual happened on each occasion, with Bone's hand letting go of the steering wheel and reaching out, his fingers fanning to comb through the thickness of my hair.

He had me come up to the drawing-room one evening after my shower. He played me Beethoven. Excerpts from the symphonies, the Furtwängler and Klemperer versions. He asked me to listen to the energy in the music, and to its terror. The new, he said, always brings profound fear to people.

'I say "new". But all his work may be a meditation on Mozart's. What d'you think?'

It wasn't the debt to Mozart, by a composer esteemed so great in his own right, which surprised me. What took me aback was being asked *my* opinion on such a complex matter.

I hummed and hawed.

'Well, I didn't know either at your age,' he said.

'You didn't?'

He laughed. 'Does that disappoint you?'

'No. Not – '

'I wasn't a prodigy. Far from it. So – you never know, Neil Pritchard ...'

Was he being serious? I stared at him; I stared for so long that he looked troubled on my account.

'It's all right, nobody's going to force you to be a musician!'

'No. I –'

He moved the stylus to the fourth movement of the Choral.

'If you can discover what's going to fulfil you,' he said, 'that's all. As I have.'

Now and then Bone gave me money, a couple of half-crowns or a ten-shilling note, which he slipped into the back pocket of my trousers.

The first time I'd been pulling my handkerchief from my pocket when the half-crowns tumbled out. Aunt Nessie bent down to pick them up. She had pressed the trousers on the ironing board the evening before, and I thought she was looking rather oddly at me.

'I got them this afternoon.'

'Mr Bone gave you them? What for?'

' "What for"? Just – for singing.'

'Well, you'd better not go throwing it about like that, son.'

'No,' I said.

'If you let me know – I can remember to thank him. Sometime.'

'Oh, I've done that.'

'But if you let me know when he gives you money …'

I said I would let Aunt Nessie know.

'You must be doing something right, mustn't you?'

After that I felt she eyed my gifts a little too brightly, as if she saw housekeeping potential there, an honorarium to augment the allowance Dad provided for my keep. Beyond the third or fourth I kept quiet about other windfalls of that sort.

It was *my* turn to pick something up.

From the paving on the terrace. A playing card, with a pattern of bright squiggles on the back. Hand-painted, I could tell by touch.

On the other side, a caricature sketch in indian ink, a giantess's head on a spindly body, roughly coloured in. The name 'Mrs Torrance' was italicised beneath, 'Happy Families'-style. I recognised the toothy, poppy-eyed features of Mrs Torrance, wife of the minister at St Kentigern's.

Bone stood holding out his hand. I passed him the card.

'Our shame is revealed.'

'You like Happy Families?' I asked him.

'I like how we play it, yes.'

'How's that?'
' "Auchendrennan Happy Families".'
'They're special cards?'
'A one-off pack,' Bone said. 'But it's a private vice.'
'Private?'
'Well, I'd hardly like it to get about. You'll kindly forget you've seen it.'
I nodded.
'Does that mean "yes", Neil?'
'Yes,' I said. 'Definitely.'

'Wait!' Bone and I were running for the sea. 'Just a moment!'
He had to slow. He placed his hands on his chest.
'You – you're too fast for me, Neil.'
But *he* had been running ahead of *me*.
I held back.
Something made me ask. 'Are you all right?'
'Yes, of course. Why – why shouldn't I be?'
I couldn't think of a reason why not.
'What's the big hurry anyway?' he said.
I shook my head, and walked beside him in silence. He was correct: this did feel a perfectly natural pace to be moving at. In time with our breathing, the comfortable pendulum swing of our arms, my easy comfortable thoughts.

I went into the cloakroom before I left Slezer's Wark for Aunt Nessie's, as I always did.
Aiming at the bowl, I looked along the shelf of books, as I always did. I knew all the titles. But today I caught the glint of glass in a frame that had been tucked behind the books.
When I'd zipped myself up, I fetched out the frame.
It held a colour photograph.
Technicolor turquoise Italian sky. Rivièra scenery, white cliffs, green sea. Bone and Maitland standing a little apart, framing – in the distance – a majestic red lighthouse.
In someone's script (Maitland's? A friend's?), '*A souvenir of the biggest erection roundabouts!!*'
I backed away.

Everything at Slezer's Wark was touched with the strange. The atmosphere wasn't hostile, but it was a very different manner of existence, exotic and seductive and out of my reach. I sensed that it was moneyed and prodigal, hedonistic and cavalier.

It was quite foreign and 'other'. But, bizarrely, I felt it was familiar to me.

I had been meant to find it.

And I knew that I secretly craved to be included in it.

When we came back to the house from our swim, we would shower.

First I stepped under the spray. And then, when I'd finished, Bone followed me.

I kept on my swimming trunks. Bone said nothing about that, and presumably put my modesty down to lower-middle-class morality. *He* stripped off, with no need of towels or pretence of forgetting I was there. It meant I was afforded a view of his hirsute nakedness from all angles.

I was too taken aback to look, to begin with. On later days I allowed myself to be more curious. I would manage to switch my eyes back when Bone was fussing with the taps or the soap, and to stare uninterrupted for a few seconds until the water ran up a mist of hot steam.

The slope of his shoulders, the curve of his back, the two globes of his buttocks. Dark hair was matted against his chest, his belly, his solid thighs. There was a small triangle of hair sketched above his bottom.

And then I homed in on it, his cock, nestling in its thick bush. I was fascinated by the alterations in its appearance: drooping or curled up or, on the contrary, twitching and starting to lose its snood of foreskin, always just a couple of seconds before the curtain was tugged fitfully along the rail.

When I wasn't at Slezer's Wark but back again in Aunt Nessie's bungalow, or just going about the streets of the town, I longed to be *there* again, in the sunny reception rooms, among the shelves of books and the geometric landscapes, in the atmosphere of learning and refinement and achievement. The '*luxe*' wasn't always '*calme*' – with Maitland present it was as if there was an overload of electricity in the air and sparks might fly at any moment – but the awkwardnesses only intensified the experience.

I took the atmosphere back to Aunt Nessie's with me. Before I left Slezer's Wark I would wash my hands in the downstairs cloakroom so that I had the smell of the soap still on my skin when I returned to Hauselock

Avenue. Sometimes I dabbed eau-de-cologne from the bottle on to my handkerchief so that I could take it out of my pocket later and be spirited back there.

In the bungalow I would sit with my aunt listening to the news or a play on the wireless. Her friends regularly called round, to play a four at whist or rummy or canasta. When the house was filled, it grew even warmer. Condensation appeared on the windows, and the rolled felt-sausages had to be pulled back from the bottoms of doors so that they could stand open. (The women's lives were a perpetual struggle against draughts, the plague of Auchendrennan. Even on summer evenings the gasfires went on at tea-time.) I would have a second supper when there was company: a couple of little sardine sandwiches, an oatcake with a slice of local red Galloway cheese on top, a macaroon, a square of millionaire's shortbread with its layer of cooking chocolate over caramel, and several cups of the best Edinburgh Blend tea. That was consolation of a kind, but I would still have preferred to be in one of those lamplit rooms at Slezer's Wark surrounded by that apple-green or white panelling hung with the work of the best names among the Scottish Colourists, listening to Furtwängler conduct Beethoven.

Surreptitiously I sniffed the back of my hand, my wrist. Now and then I could detect the smoky traces of cigars or Egyptian cigarettes caught in the weave of my pullover cuffs and arms, and that too would sustain me at odd points through an evening alone with Aunt Nessie or listening in my bedroom to her friends talking and laughing behind the thin dividing wall.

I heard some of Aunt Nessie's friends discussing Maitland.

That his siblings disapproved of Bone, for all his growing fame as a composer and being talked about as next Hygh Musik Makar to our Queen. That they were afraid of what might happen to their brother's share of the Maitland inheritance. That they thought there were too many spongers and parasites, and why didn't their hosts just give them the heave-ho. That none of his family enjoyed this music Bone wrote, which was supposed to be something special, and (embarrassingly to them) dedicated to Douglas Maitland.

A few breaths later Aunt Nessie's regulars were telling her that I was on to a good thing there. Aunt Nessie said, not very confidently, that she imagined it was useful experience for me.

'Keeps him from getting under your feet, Nessie. But off the streets too.'

'He's not that kind of boy.'

One of her friends giggled at the remark, but no one else saw the humour in it.

'Still, it's interesting for you to hear about, Nessie. Getting the story from the inside.'

'Oh yes,' Aunt Nessie replied, in a downturned tone of voice. Now she was sounding less and less sure about what had seemed so propitious and a feather in her cap just a few moments before.

'Is he a clever lad, Nessie?'

'Och yes. Kay's told me he is. He's at a good school, right enough.'

'Well, then. No doubt he can handle it.'

Silence.

Aunt Nessie spoke first.

'Any more for any more tea, girls?'

★

I felt I might have sung for hours.

" – following my leader from one group to another – "

My voice had a *cleansed* quality to it.

" – groping in slippery tangle from the wreck of ships – "

It arose quite effortlessly.

" – wading in pools after the abominable creatures of the sea – "

I believed I could have dealt with any complexity of notes asked of me.

" – and ever with an eye cast backward – "

My voice wrapped itself around the music. The two were inseparable, indivisible.

Making my way down the drive I passed a box of emptied wine bottles from a recent dinner party. I picked one up. The name on the label was extravagantly improbable; I knew I'd never remember it, and so I covered the bottle with my pullover and kept on walking.

Back at Aunt Nessie's I washed off the label and dried it very carefully with a towel.

HORSTEINER ABTSBERG-REUCHSBERG Riesling

I supposed it was what the smart set drank back in London, where the wine must have been sent from. Now I had a small but actual memento of their evening, a keepsake. Even if the name was to vanish from *their* recollection in time, it wouldn't from mine, I would be the curator of its glamour.

I accidentally knocked the spoon off my saucer.

We both bent down at the same time to pick it up. I heard my knees cracking.

Bone reached out first. Our hands collided.

I tried to take hold of the spoon. In the process I touched his fingers again.

We were still bent over. He looked at me through his unruly fringe of hair. I looked straight back into his eyes. His violet eyes with the long lashes.

Bone started to rise, drawing himself straighter. I did likewise.

My eyes were finding it hard to focus. I was burning hot. I looked away.

I picked up my cup, and gulped down some tea.

Out the corner of my eye I saw him move away, stand silently with his back to me looking at one of the paintings on the wall, where he must have been trying to get a better view of the situation reflected in the frame's glass.

14

I walked into the kitchen at lunchtime. Aunt Nessie looked up and noticed her girdle hanging from the pulley, and grabbed at it. Then she slipped the letter she'd been reading behind the bread crock.

'Have you managed to meet anyone else yet? I mean, your own age?'

Funny time to be asking me that.

'Not really,' I said.

'We must be – '

She patted her perm as she passed the little wall mirror, not entirely believing what she was saying.

' – rather dull company for you, Neil. Still – there's Mr Bone. And once you get back to Glasgow …'

Then she must have realised she'd said too much by mentioning Glasgow.

'I'll cut us some bread for our lunch, shall I?'

The telephone started to ring out in the hall. Aunt Nessie put down the bread knife.

'That'll be Jean Shearer.'

'I'll get the bread,' I said.

'She picks her moments, doesn't she? There's tea in the pot, Neil.'

When she'd gone, I pulled the letter out from behind the crock. I recognised my mother's handwriting.

> *I'm sorry if it's going to be a burden to you, but just*
> *until the end of the month. Then the school term begins*
> *and he won't notice so much. Eric and I are trying to do*
> *this like two sensible adults. We've taken the decision, so*
> *that's that. Neil will learn to cope somehow, young folk*
> *at that age –*

I heard the telephone receiver being replaced on its cradle. I quickly pushed the sheets of paper back behind the bread crock.

The kitchen floor had an unsteady feel to it, a roll, as if I was walking across the deck of a ship. A listing ship without a captain or a pilot.

Bone had me come across to the piano.

He stood behind me, to explain something on the manuscript page. I felt the warmth of his breath on the back of my neck. As he reached his arm out in front of me my stomach tightened, a sensation of locked sight gripped me.

'Am I interrupting?' Maitland called over from the door.

'Why would you be doing that?' Bone asked, quickly taking a couple of steps forward.

'I don't want to spoil the mood – '

'Which mood is that?'

' – the creative process. When it's in full spate – '

'You're not.'

' – and all the creative juices have got going.'

Bone looked briefly from Maitland to me, and then back at Maitland. He gave him an affable, compliant smile.

'Our Edinburgh friends. On the phone. "For Euan, please".'

Bone's smile faded.

'For *me*?'

'They must think yours truly's got the makings of a turncoat.'

'Why on earth – ?' Bone asked.

'That's the psychology, I expect.'

★

'Here – '

From behind her back Aunt Nessie produced a cream cookie on a plate. She put the plate down in front of me.

'I was in an extravagant mood,' she said. 'From Gavigan's. Go ahead. Indulge yourself!'

I thanked her.

The two halves of the cookie were soft and yielding, as they should have been. The brilliantly white whisked cream was smooth and sweet, as it should have been. The top of the cookie was dusted liberally with flour and caster sugar, just as it should have been.

A paragon of cream cookies.

I tried to make it last.

'Is it all right? Nothing wrong with it, is there?'

Aunt Nessie liked to see me eat up, which meant not letting anything linger too long on the plate. I didn't want to offend her.

'It's lovely,' I said.

She had bought me the cream cookie for a noble reason, because she was sorry for me, because she saw that – a little further off – I couldn't be spared suffering.

★

Mrs Faichnie was out of sorts. We had a visitor, but not the asked-for sort.

I was pushed into the recess of empty space beneath the staircase.

The visitor emerged from the music room, accompanied by Maitland.

'... Then I'll leave you to your composing, Mr Bone.'

A tall woman in a tweed suit and four strings of pearls, and flat lacing shoes on her large feet. She had a long, narrow, masculine face; in her colouring and her manner of holding her head high I saw a resemblance to Maitland.

She was looking for somewhere to stub out her cigarette, and to Mrs Faichnie's evident disgust she dropped it into a vase of lilies. But a Maitland Valkyrie wasn't to be challenged, and Mrs Faichnie squeezed out a smile for her – a sour pickled smile.

Bone and I had another 'excursion' planned for this afternoon.

Before we set out I went into the cloakroom.

Maitland came downstairs looking for Bone, and found him in the hall.

I put off flushing the cistern.

The 'Blessed Virgin', as Maitland called his sister, had been down to stir up trouble. The rest of the family had probably put her up to it, wanted to know just how much it was costing to sate two men's sensual appetites.

'How much you're spending on *me*, you mean?' Bone said.

'Of course not on you. I could spend just as much on myself.'

'So, what are we proving? This way two can live as cheaply as one?'

'Oh, not "living". Not according to the BV. This is lying down in the slough of iniquity. We're doing as the bloody reptiles do. Or pigs, is it? Rolling in our own filth.'

'What if she's right?'

'She doesn't know a fucking thing about us. Or about anything. She's a smug, Presbyterian, man-hating virgin. *They* don't count.'

The voices grew fainter. I pulled the plug, and wished I was flushing *that* woman's head down the Armitage Shanks.

I'd got ahead of Bone, running for the sea.

'Neil!'

I didn't look round.

'*Neil!*'

I continued running. Was I going too fast again?

'*Stop*, Neil!'

His voice was ripping. The sound slowed me. I looked back.

He wasn't where I was expecting to see him.

I stopped.

Bone was still running, and pointing at something.

I looked across.

'The flag!'

The red flag. I hadn't seen it.

'Come back here!'

I started to run again, towards Bone. Suddenly the sand felt treacherously soft and unstable beneath me. I took seven-league-boot strides, flying jumps.

'For Christ's sake, Neil!'

'I'm all right,' I said.

'Didn't you – ' He was fighting to get his breath back. ' – didn't you *see* the flag?'

'I'm okay.'

'Only just. The sands out there – you *know* what they're like. The Lair – '

Why was he so angry with me?

'I'm supposed to chase after you, am I? And get us both drowned?'

'I didn't *get* drowned, though.'

'What about The Lantern Bearers? What would I have done then?'

The frigging 'Lantern Bearers'! For a few seconds I was just as angry as him.

'Neil, Neil!' He stood ruffling my hair. I had an instinct to duck – but I didn't.

His hand slipped down to the nape of my neck.

I had terrified him.

91

'I'm sorry,' I heard myself saying.

'It's all right, it's all right. C'mon. Let's try and forget it.'

He pointed where to go, where we should have been in the first place if I hadn't lost my way, to the stretch of shore where the bathing was safe.

'C'mon!' he said. 'I'll race you!'

I hesitated. But a couple of seconds later I'd set off in pursuit.

★

'It's me, Aunt Nessie!'

Already from the back door I could see that where she was standing – in front of the hall-stand mirror – her colour was high.

Another hot flush, I supposed.

'Mr McLuskie dropped in with that.'

She nodded through to the kitchen table.

'He's lending you it.'

A book. *Further Memories*. By Robert Louis Stevenson.

'Why's he lending it to me?'

'You'd better ask *him* that. He just said it was something he'd always had in the house.'

Maybe it wasn't whizzing hormones to blame for Aunt Nessie's red face. Her eyes were shiny too, and a blue vein shaped like a tiny forked twig was twitching in her temple. When she had her flushes, she clutched a Swiss hanky tightly inside her perspiring hand; it was still obtruding, unnoticed, from her cardigan cuff.

'Do I have to read it?'

'That's up to you, Neil.'

'Do you think I should read it?'

'I don't think anything about it.'

They were essays.

'The Lantern Bearers' was included.

The book's index didn't whet my curiosity much.

> *Three Walking Tours*
> *Memories of Fontainebleau*
> *Swiss Notes*
> *Early Sketches*
> *Fragments*

I took the book to bed. I turned to 'A Chapter on Dreams', which followed 'The Lantern Bearers'. I read by the light of the little lamp on the table, but I wasn't able to read for long before my eyelids grew heavy

The book fell from my hands and somersaulted on to the floor. I left it.

The dreamlife summoned me, and I hoped it wouldn't be Glasgow but somewhere much closer to me now, that white-harled aberration of a house among the town's prosaic grey. Slezer's Wark. If I could find an open door to enter by, or – failing that – a window, or even a chimney to go sliding down …

15

Two o'clock.

The front door was on the latch.

Bone called downstairs to me.

'Come on up for a few minutes, Neil.'

He was alone in the house. There was a record playing on the hi-fi. He was sitting – lying back in the feather cushions of the sofa – staring up at the ceiling.

I asked what he was listening to.

'Brahms.'

'Not Beethoven?'

He passed me the record sleeve.

The eighteen Liebeslieder-Walzer. Opus 52.

'Splendid stuff,' he said.

Four voices – two men, two women – sounding as if they were gathered round a piano in a Vienna salon. They sang with the native lilt of the waltz.

I pulled out the page of lyrics, found the translation.

> *A little bird flies through the skies,*
> *searching for a branch;*
> *thus does one heart seek another,*
> *where it might rest in bliss.*

It wasn't really what I would have expected Bone to be listening to. I watched him settle back in the sofa, with his hand supporting his head. He shut his eyes to hear better, to *be* there, at the recording: in the Brahmsaal, Wien, on 15 November 1947.

Irmgard Seefried and Elisabeth Höngen. Hugo Meyer-Welfing and Hans Hotter. And the two accompanists.

> *The foliage trembles*
> *where a bird in flight*
> *has brushed against it.*
> *And so my soul*
> *trembles too, shuddering*
> *with love, desire and pain,*
> *whenever it thinks of you.*

94

The folk poetry was simple, but the melodies were ingeniously seductive. So sweet, and so sad.

A salon entertainment. But somehow, I recognised, it could tell of all the love and despair that was possible in a person's life.

★

'What was London like?' I asked.

We were up by the Black Rocks. Bone was lying stretched out in his swimming briefs and t-shirt. He opened his eyes.

'London?'

'What was it like living there?'

'Why d'you ask that?'

'I was wondering.'

'Oh ... it might be another life now.'

'Did you like it?'

'Yes. Yes, I did.'

'Why?'

' "Why"?' he repeated.

I nodded.

'Oh ...' He sighed. 'There was so much to do.'

'What sort of things?'

'Concerts. People to see. Restaurants. Clubs. You could find anything to buy.'

'Auchendrennan must be ...'

I didn't go on. Bone shrugged.

'You assume it's the centre of the universe,' he said, ' London, when you're there.'

'Isn't it?'

'Life moves us on.'

'Do you miss it?' I asked him

'I think about it, certainly.'

'You remember it?'

'Oh yes, I remember.'

He didn't tell me just what he remembered.

A few months later I would put together a geography for myself from magazines.

Bone's and Maitland's London, as it was and as it became, the one where
I felt they really belonged.

Fifty-Five Jermyn Street

Bistro 51

The American Bar at the Savoy

Bloom's Delicatessen (only on Tuesdays)

King Bomba in Soho

Cromwellian Discotheque

Jackson's of Piccadilly

Les Ambassadeurs Turkish baths

The Clermont casino

Denman and Goddard, Sulka

Morris Stanton's barbershop

Grumbles bistro

McRoberts and Tunnard's previews

(Elegant lunchtimes, swishy evenings.

Striped awnings, cut flowers. The coral glow of little table-lamps.

Doormen with umbrellas; running between a revolving door and the
open door of a taxi cab.)

Lilleman & Cox for dry cleaning

Heywood Hill for books

Berry Bros & Rudd for wine

Fribourg & Treyer for cigarettes

Pulbrook & Gould for flowers

'You don't go back?'

'No.'

It couldn't be because they couldn't afford to go back. Had they fallen
out with the people they'd known then?

'Is it too painful?'

'Why "painful"?'

'I don't know.'

I thought I might have said too much.

'I've had to grow up a bit, that's all. It was a bit of a fairytale living there.
Not – not quite real.'

We fell silent.

When I looked again Bone had closed his eyes.

I let my own eyes pass across his body. His surprisingly muscular arms,

96

with their dark hairs earlier smoothed in one direction by the water. His legs, strong rather than well-shaped. His thighs, where the hair was coarser. The calves.

My eyes travelled back up. I kept for last his swimming trunks. They were yellow. With a bulge in front. Some curly hairs escaped from beneath the elastic that held everything in place.

I was lying on my side, directly in line with his groin, no more than eighteen inches from him. I felt my own cock stirring inside my bathing trunks. I shifted awkwardly, enjoying the friction against the taut material of my trunks but also alarmed. I pulled at my t-shirt, but it wouldn't stretch any further.

The sun grew a little stronger, it turned the hairs on his knees golden, to furze. I looked at my own thin, stubbornly hairless legs, and then back at his, and I tried to imagine living – as he did – inside that body, always having that breathtaking view of myself whenever I glanced proudly down.

I held my breath. I felt a raw, sore pressure in my groin, pulses of pain that were also intensely pleasurable. I closed my eyes to concentrate.

When I opened my eyes, Bone was looking at me, observing my face. I stared back at him for two or three seconds. I rolled over on to my other side.

Had he seen anything else?

I felt my face firing. My neck. The back of my neck.

He was still looking, I could tell, I had the sensation of his eyes on the nape of my neck, on my right shoulder, on the top of my head, my right ear.

I turned round, because I couldn't bear it any longer. But he looked away. He pulled himself forward on the rock, placed his hands flat and pushed hard on them to get up on to his feet. On his sturdy legs again he had firm, sure balance.

I waited until he'd jumped down on to the sand and was stooping forward to look at some worm-casts (was he *really* interested?) before I followed him. I wasn't so steady on my own legs, and almost fell over as I prepared to jump off. He half-turned round with his arm stretched out and his hand open, but I aimed for a spot on the wet sand a couple of yards away.

I landed with a heavy squelch. I stared behind me at the marks of my bare feet in the sand. It looked like the point where a boy might have disappeared, sunk down into the underworld.

16

Isa Gilhooly had been in the surgery waiting-room.

She'd heard Dr Joss's voice outside, he breenged in, as was his wont, ignoring all the commonplace patients waiting for the other two doctors.

'Is the Slezer's Wark prescription made up yet?' he barked out.

There was a new girl at the desk, and she rolled her eyes and said something about 'not yet', and Joss looked daggers at her.

'It's for Mr Bone. And I don't call Quinidine an idle matter,' he said.

'Quinidine', Isa had quite distinctly heard the word, and Joss declaiming it as if he was Laurence Olivier himself.

'What's that for?' Aunt Nessie asked her.

Isa had looked it up in a medical dictionary in the Library. It was given out for heart tremors and palpitations.

The two women stared at each other. Then they turned and looked at me.

I immediately dropped my eyes to my book. *Ring of Bright Water*, which I had taken off one of the two small bookshelves in Aunt Nessie's living-room. I didn't care tuppence for otters, but I needed cover – *my* camouflage, just as bloody otters had theirs – in order to digest Isa Gilhooly's information.

I couldn't connect tremors and palpitations with Bone. It was older people who gave any thought to their hearts. Bone was younger than either of my parents. He dressed in white linen and sandals with bare feet, I saw his long trailing stylish white duster coat hanging up in the cloak-room, he walked quickly and swam in Dalquhirk Bay. So the tablets might as well have been diagnosed for someone else, another man, not for this Euan Bone *I* knew.

★

Between two pages in the middle of *Further Memories* I found the receipt of Mr McLuskie's purchase.

He'd bought it in a second-hand bookshop, the one in Coulter Street, three days before he'd given it to me.

So much for it having come off a shelf in his own house.

The situation was a little cloudier than I had thought.

★

I took some of Bone's money to Murray's hardware shop and I spent it on a torch.

A red and silver Aurora Junior, with a spare battery. The owner Mr Murray let it roam over the shelves of polish and nail jars at the back of the dark shop.

'This'll keep you out of mischief, young man.'

'Start you off, more like,' his cheeky daughter said out of his hearing, from behind the grille where I had to pay. 'Will you be wanting a poke for that?'

'What?'

'A paper bag.'

I told her not to bother, thank you.

'Suit yourself. Just don't go shining that thing where you shouldn't. Like down Lovers' Loan.'

I backed away. Was she any friend of that new girl in the doctors' surgery, I wondered.

I turned and pulled on the handle of the unwieldy door, the buzzer cackled, and I hurried out on to the street, banging a couple of the brooms that hung for sale outside against the window glass.

★

Today I was required to be terrified. First the crazed fisher-wife, who slit her throat at Canty Bay on too much drink – and how I watched the breathing body being carted down the Quadrant. And then, glimpsed in a house in the same Quadrant, the 'dark old woman' who continued to live alone with the corpse of her last visitor.

" – in the dread hour of the dusk, as we were clambering on the garden-walls, she opened a window in that house of mortality – and cursed us – "

I was immobilised in horror on C-sharp, while the piano churned a bass beneath me.

" – cursed us in a shrill voice and with a marrowy choice of language – "

We jumped forward three or four manuscript pages, to reach the sea storm. The elements exploded, as if (Bone explained to me) some vast passion were spilling over: whether it was God's fury or nature's challenge. A shuddering tremolando on the piano was strangely modulated into an E-flat arpeggio, lacking the fifth B-flat.

'We're held by these great forces, Neil. There's nothing we can do except surrender, hope for mercy – '

After that, the stalwart figures stood braving the fierce spray on the harbour wall for a sight of the lost fishing boat. I only had a little to do while Bone reconsidered the piano part. A clamour of quavers, then a sudden reduction in scale, from F down to D-flat major.

The afternoon left us both, but especially Bone, worn out. While the rest of Auchendrennan had been going about its trite business, we had soared to glorious heights and trawled infernal depths.

'Wednesday *morning*, Neil. How's that?'
'And the afternoon too?'
'Afternoon, no-can-do.'
'The morning's fine,' I said.
'Nine till eleven? That's okay by you?'
'Okay by me.'
As if it wouldn't have been.
'Thanks, Neil. I appreciate it.'

Wednesday, noon.

I'd come through from my bedroom to the kitchen. Aunt Nessie was out in the garden, checking on the washing that was drying on the line.

She stopped at one of the sheets from my bed. She went closer, stretched the sheet at one part, and for several moments inspected the surface. She let the sheet go, smoothed it with her hand, watched it gently fill with breeze, and walked on to where she'd pegged out her underclothes, furthest from the house and where I – or our neighbour Mr McLuskie – might have only a long chance of seeing.

After lunch I helped Aunt Nessie in the garden. Then, when she retired inside for Woman's Hour on the wireless and a nap at the same time, I went off on my own, to do a circuit or two of the town.

I had a prickly encounter with some of the local boys. I came upon them sitting on top of a wall. One of the gang, with his quiff of carrot hair, gave me a wolf-whistle as I slinked past; the others sniggered.

'We see you – '

I didn't stop, although the voices wanted me to.

' – going up and down Yett Street.'

I tried not to go faster or slower.

'Up and down!' they chanted. 'Up and down!'

'Like a whore's drawers,' someone said.

Laughter.

'Always going in there, aren't you? In and out, in and out!'

More laughter. It was meant to sound mocking and cruel.

'We know.'

They couldn't know. (Keep walking, Pritchard.) Because I didn't know myself. (Keep walking, don't stop.)

The ringleader with red hair was singing. I recognised Bone's 'Pleugh Sang'. He was exaggerating the rhythms, and using a fol-de-rol voice, making each note sound out of true.

A gob of angry spit just missed me by inches. That was all the warning I needed.

People were passing by and I was spared worse. I continued walking away. The boy with red hair went on singing, though. I heard it until I'd turned the corner: the abuse at Bone was all the keener for the song being mauled by someone who'd had to study hard to learn it in the first place.

After that I kept clear of the old hilly streets with their cobbled wynds where, conceivably, more of the town lads could have been lying in ambush for me. I gave them a wide berth, and persuaded myself I was reconnoitering this afternoon into those other peripheral corners of Auchendrennan I hadn't had time to scout round before.

They didn't keep me away from Yett Street, though.

I was walking along the opposite pavement when I saw, distantly, the figure of a man appear from the canopy of rhododendrons on the driveway and paddle past the gatepost with his hand.

I stopped by an archway into a joiner's yard, where I'd once noticed fresh coffins standing in a shed.

The figure walked quickly along the side of the street that was in shadow.

101

He was younger than Bone. His shoulders were too broad for the cut of the jacket, and he flexed them, which caused the jacket to ride up and wrinkle at his elbows.

He made a clean right turn, as if he knew the lay-out of the town well, into one of the sandy lanes down to the shore.

I ran after him.

Fifteen or twenty yards ahead he kicked at a stone, two stones, three, and appeared thankful to be out-of-doors again. He started to whistle, a few bars of a pop song, then he stopped.

He let his legs run away with him, down a path between two dunes.

He stopped again.

First he looked to his right, in the direction of Slezer's Wark. Then he looked to the left, towards the harbour.

He hunkered down on a large stone.

I approached closer.

He reached into his inside pocket and extracted an envelope. He looked in, checked the contents. He might have been counting something – money. Then he pushed the envelope back into his pocket, and stood up. He fastened the jacket's middle button, and burrowed his hands into his trouser pockets. The suit looked more ill-fitting than ever, exactly the sort of townie garb to get him noticed in Auchendrennan.

He turned round. He aimed the toe of his shoe at a plastic cup, left behind from a picnic, and it went skittering across the sand. His face – quite handsome, but in a sharp and foxy way – was fixed in thought. The envelope, I noticed, made a bulge under his jacket. I could see the outline of his thighs where the fabric of the trousers pulled over them, and the rounds of his buttocks at the rear – even the crease itself – where the seam was drawn very taut. His socks were worn thin at the heels.

He had powerful shoulders and a solid neck, and he looked quite different from those pale and intellectual young men with their quickfire wit whom Bone and Maitland now and then entertained.

What had been the purpose of *his* visit to Slezer's Wark? And why had Bone thought it necessary to postpone our customary afternoon in the music room?

Hands still buried in his trouser pockets, the caller rounded the next dune and went walking up the ramp of sand with a more purposeful turn of speed, heading for another of those sand-scattered, unmade side-lanes which, like the dank cobbled back wynds in the harbour quarter, were the town's secret geography.

The next afternoon I didn't report to Slezer's Wark.

I wasn't ill. I had no less desire to sing.

Perhaps it was my revenge.

I left Aunt Nessie's as usual. When I reached the end of the avenue, however, I turned left and not right. I was dressed for Slezer's Wark, in my best going-out clothes, as Aunt Nessie insisted that I should. If I hadn't put them on, the same clothes which I always wore in the afternoon, she would have plied me with questions.

I didn't know where to go. Anywhere except where I was expected. As I ran west, away from the town in the direction of Dalquhirk beach, I kept glancing at my Timex, so that I could picture the anxiety, then the irritation which I was bound to be causing. I saw the piano with its lid raised and its teeth bared. I saw Bone turning the pages of a newspaper, unable to concentrate on more than a couple of sentences at a time, turning to the next page, and the next. Mrs Faichnie would have put her head round the corner of the door, to check. 'Should I be ringing about the lad, Mr Bone?' Bone would shake his head, cultivating his annoyance, letting it build inside him until he was ready to take it out on someone or something.

I was the one responsible, but I felt oddly guiltless as I went racing to find somewhere else to be. Life had gone on without me in that house for five or six summers before this one, and if Bone didn't have the patience to cope now – with this small neglect on my part – then that was his problem, I couldn't help that.

I ended up in Rosmailzie Forest. I shouted up into the trees. I threw some pine cones, and dislodged more, which came tumbling down through layers of branches. I wandered on inside. Briefly I lost my way, I couldn't get my bearings. My heart thumped inside my chest, and waves of feebleness passed through my legs. I couldn't hear any footsteps on the soft floor of loam and needles, and I didn't have my torch with me, but at last I came to a scatter of pine cones and realised that this was where I'd been earlier, where I'd begun. From there I was able to retrace my footsteps, from the impressions of them marked in the ground – and then, after that, I made my escape, without looking back.

When I returned to Slezer's Wark the next day, Friday, I told Bone I'd had a stomach bug. I knew he hadn't phoned Aunt Nessie, so he couldn't be certain if I was speaking the truth or not.

I didn't apologise. Bone, unshaved, looked vexed with me. His voice was a little higher and tighter than usual, but he had no intention of giving in to me, of saying it had been a wasted three hours for him and why in God's name hadn't I thought to get in touch?

I sang well that afternoon. Bone had two days' worth of work to crowd into one single session. Tea was brought to us as usual, but had to be drunk cold. At half-past four Mrs Faichnie found an excuse to come in – to fetch the tray of tea things – which reminded Bone that he was obliged to stop now. With a show of reluctance he gathered his loose manuscript pages together.

'We *could* go on,' I heard myself suggesting. 'If you want to – '

He paused before flicking back through the sheaf of pages. He didn't thank me or enquire if this would put my aunt out. He picked up his pencil and started entering black crotchets in the treble clef. He found the notes on the piano. I sang them, so-tee-fah. He turned to the typed pages of annotated Stevenson text.

'What do I keep? What can I lose?'

He asked me, could I please read?

"There – there the coats would be unbuttoned and the bull's-eye disclosed; and in the chequering glimmer, under the huge windy hall of the night – "

I thought I was reading badly. I glanced over. Bone was listening intently.

'Keep reading. I want to hear it in *your* voice. *You* have to say it, Neil.'

" – and cheered by a rich steam of toasting tinware, those fortunate young gentlemen would crouch together in the cold sand of the links – "

'No, it's surplus, this. Go on.'

" – or on the scaly bilges of the fishing boat, and delight themselves with inappropriate talk – "

'Skip to the last sentence in that section, will you. About bliss.'

"The essence of this bliss – "

'That's it!'

" – was to walk by yourself in the black night – "

'*This* next bit coming …'

He walked over to the piano, sat down. He had written out this long final sentence for himself.

'Continue, Neil.'

But this time *he* read it aloud too, our two voices proceeding in unison. A man's and a boy's.

" – the slide shut; the top-coat buttoned; not a ray escaping, whether to conduct your footsteps or to make your glory public: a mere pillar of darkness in the dark; and all the while, deep down in the privacy of your fool's heart, to know you had a bull's-eye at your belt, and to exult and sing over the knowledge – "

I stopped. He repeated the last words solo.

" – to exult and sing over the knowledge – "

He sat staring ahead of him, towards the window. His lips continued to move, but this time repeating the words only to himself, in silence.

17

I didn't want the summer to ever end.

A letter reached me from home, an anodyne letter filled with evasions. I hadn't been prepared to find it waiting for me on the breakfast table. Already I was starting to lose my focus on that unhappy domestic scenario. My father and mother were presumably picking over their marriage, detail by excruciating detail. I was grateful now to have that distance between myself and Glasgow. Even the 'arrangements' at Aunt Nessie's didn't seem so bad by comparison.

★

After our next two swims Bone didn't suggest that we shower off the brine. I wanted everything to continue to be just the same, if it could be, and I was sorry for any changes.

Why did we *not* shower now? I first, and then he following?

★

I opened the book Mr McLuskie had lent me, and found 'The Lantern Bearers'.

I read ahead.

The later portions turn to the subject of literary forms. Stevenson chastises novelists for toning life down to the grey and monochrome and matter-of-fact, for supplying such lacklustre so-called heroes. Have they forgotten the vivid colours life once had for them?

'They have been boys and youths; they have lingered outside the window of the beloved, who was then most probably writing to someone else; they have sat before a sheet of paper, and felt themselves mere continents of congested poetry, not one line of which would flow; they have walked alone in the woods; they have been to sea, they have hated, they have feared, they have longed to knife a man, and maybe done it; the wild taste of life has stung their palate.'

I read the passage through again, to its commanding final nine words.

' – the wild taste of life has stung their palate.'

Bone hadn't made any mention of that section to me. None of it appeared on the typed sheet of intended lyrics. But I felt I could understand its poetry very well for myself.

★

The telephone rang late one evening. Aunt Nessie looked up with alarm. Only bad news travelled so late, after ten o'clock.

She got up and went out into the hall, closing the door behind her. I followed her to the door and stood a couple of inches from it, which was close enough for me to hear. I caught the first mention of 'Kay'. Aunt Nessie was saying this and that, to try to calm my mother, but it was against an unstoppable tide of marital recriminations.

'You don't know, though. You can't be certain, can you?'

Which was exactly the goad my mother needed.

I still didn't feel easy with a telephone. The black bakelite had an unfriendly, sinister look to it. For some reason its posture put me in mind of a frog's: a mournful and spiteful *toad*.

The instrument didn't serve us well.

Sometimes my mother would take it into her head to call my father at the air base. She would be put through to his office, and always found herself talking to a woman subordinate.

'And *you* are Miss …?' she would enquire with the pretence of forgetfulness. 'Oh, "*Mrs*", is it? I'm so sorry. Yes, of course – '

Of course nothing.

There was a rapid turn-over of typists, and it was difficult for my mother to keep track. She would ask my father about them, and he would look puzzled, either by her interest or by the effort to remember if he had told her that the last one had been replaced a couple of months back. (He *looked* puzzled, but I could do the same when I stood in front of a mirror and practised the facial motions.)

My mother was keen to hear the women's voices, so that from their accents she could place where they came from, geographically and socially. My father would tell her 'yes' or 'no' or 'maybe' or 'I haven't thought about it really'.

107

My mother *heard* the women while my father, sitting at our dining-table, was also able to picture them to himself. I only ever met a couple of them, and they both struck me as being the dreary-Deirdre type; they might have been typical, but naturally my mother couldn't take that for granted. Perhaps the latest recruit to the Remington ranks looked like – like Sabrina? Or even like Diana Dors? It must have been a constant fancy and fear for her, and because there was never a definite answer to hand it became an obsession to try to discover.

Hearing no more than the voice over the phone couldn't reassure her. She did go to an Officers' Mess Dance at the air base every Christmas, but that was only once a year, and it wasn't possible to tell who was not invited or discreetly encouraged not to attend those Air Force public relations exercises.

★

' "Beware the heat o' the sun".'

I opened my eyes and looked up from the deck-chair.

Maitland was standing in front of me, paying me very close attention.

'Mr Maitland? I – I'm sorry – ?'

Bone had asked me to have tea by myself, outside if I wanted, while he went off to make a few phone calls.

Maitland had set out earlier to collect the Facel from the Forge Garage, where it was being serviced.

'I wasn't expecting ...'

'That's all right. Don't get up. It's your privilege. Tea and a seat. Don't you get bloody exhausted standing so long?'

Maitland's manner puzzled me, and his wrinkled shirt-collar and untidy tie.

'I get to sit sometimes,' I said.

'Rather you than me.'

'It's just, I wasn't expecting – '

'Yes, all right, lad, you've told me that.'

I got to my feet. Maitland shot the metallic blue sky an affronted look.

'Whew! It's turned very hot.'

'Yes,' I said. 'It has.'

' "The heat o' the sun". As I mentioned, did I not?'

'Yes, Mr Maitl– '

'Sounds Italian. Or Greek, or something.'

(Gin, was it to blame? Or whisky?)

'Not that Icarus,' he continued, 'knew any better, didn't know the first bloody thing about it. Clean forgot.'

(Why Icarus?)

'But for us – it's mad dogs. And Englishmen. Or – or should I say – ' He coughed some phlegm into his handkerchief. ' – Anglo-Scotsmen. Fits the bill better. Going out and about. In the mid-day ...'

' "Sun"?' I prompted him.

'The sun. Yes.'

He wandered away, leaving me with a vague and misdirected smile.

From the deck-chair I squinted up at a few high fluffy clouds. I knew for myself not to look too close to the sun.

'The heat'? But he wasn't warning me about my complexion, was he?

At the very instant I was picturing to myself a mad black one – a dog actually started barking down on the shore.

Warnings cease to be so, I could understand, if they come too late.

The dog continued to bark. Every sound carried extra significance in the stillness and heat. The barking seemed to be fretting against my brain, making it ache.

18

I heard a cello playing.

I thought it must be Maitland. But when I was shown into the hall Maitland was on the downstairs phone enquiring about train connections to Edinburgh.

Mrs Faichnie left me in the music room. She tended to accompany me through when she felt she was unappreciated by the others, or hadn't been consulted about a guest's arrival, when she was needing to assert herself.

'You wait here now.'

What else was I to do?

The door was ajar. I stayed close by, listening for Bone's approach. I heard footsteps on the staircase. Maitland put down the phone. Someone laughed on the staircase, either Bone or the third man.

The guest was young, elegantly panther-like in black clothes, but with a shock of beach-bum's blond sun-bleached hair. It was the Parisian look, sartorially speaking; but he spoke with an Australian twang.

The cellist, again. Paul Quigley.

'This has been a *real* once-in-a-lifetime.'

'We'll make it a party-time next time,' Bone said.

Maitland fetched the visitor's black trenchcoat.

'I would take you to the station myself,' Maitland told him, 'but I've a heap of correspondence to deal with.'

A car horn blew, the taxi.

'And sadly,' Bone said, 'I have an appointment with Mr Stevenson.'

'Not "sadly"?' the young man asked, with a very eager smile.

'No. You're right. I *enjoy* these afternoons. They do leave me pretty whacked, I have to say.'

More politesse; but a chilly sort from Maitland.

When the guest had gone and the front door had been closed, Maitland stood glaring at Bone.

'And what does *that* look mean, Douglas?'

'Rather an empty vessel, Mr Quigley, I should've thought.'

'It was you he came to see.'

'So he said. Inviting himself indeed.'

'Cellists' chat.'

'It was *you* he was listening to. Everything you said, hung on to every word. A proper little disciple you've got yourself there, Euan.'

'Didn't you think he played well?'

Maitland turned to the staircase. 'I defer judgement.'

'Your classes must've made a great – '

'Don't try to fob me off that way, Euan. I was a very convenient excuse for him.'

'Excuse for what?'

'As if you didn't know – '

Bone was calling upstairs after Maitland. 'For God's sake, Douglas!'

'Keep your voice down. The boy – '

Bone turned round. But I pirouetted on my ankles faster. By the time he reached the door and came into the room, I was over near the window, looking outside quite nonchalantly. The door was closed. I pretended to start at the sound, and angled my head round.

'Oh, Mr Bone. I didn't hear you.'

He gave me a smile, full of the disbelief I was due.

The subject of the visit was still preoccupying Maitland the next day.

Bone and I were taking tea outside, in the sun. Maitland appeared. I had heard him earlier, practising upstairs.

'Do join us, Douglas,' Bone said. 'Just deserts.'

'What for?'

'Your playing, of course.'

'It was bloody awful. You know it was.'

'That's nonsense.'

'Were you trying to show me up yesterday?'

'Douglas – '

Bone nodded over at me.

'I'm going for a walk,' Maitland said.

'Wait for me,' Bone said.

'Don't you two want to celebrate?'

'Celebrate what?'

'Another page and a half under your belts?'

'Neil will have to celebrate alone.'

While Bone gulped down the remaining tea in his cup, Maitland allowed himself to look grateful. I thought it was possible he was going to shed tears, but that danger passed. He merely bowed his head, nodded.

It also occurred to me – it struck home – that we were going through a volatile phase, and that this was really only a truce.

'See the big full moon last night, son?' Mrs Faichnie asked me, and that was as far as she would permit herself to comment.

Maitland had another source of irritation.

He opened the music room door next afternoon without knocking.

'La Grizel's on the blower. Tried telling her you were busy, but she was sure you'd make an exception for *her*.'

'I know what it's about.'

'Some state secret, is it?'

Bone looked up at me, and nodded towards the armchair.

'Is it, Euan?'

'Of course not.'

'Well, then?'

'She was going to see a doctor,' Bone said.

Maitland, arms folded, leaned against the door jamb.

'Why's she phoning *you*? Has she some good news you have to know too?'

'For God's sake, Douglas! It's Grizel we're talking about.'

Grizel Langmuir, who had opened the door to Miss Pettigrew and me that very first day. And a kind of talisman for me.

(Aunt Nessie, fishing for what I might be able to tell *her*, had recounted a little background.)

Her father had been a composer, well-considered in his day for a series of lush landscape pieces featuring different corners of Scotland. Bone had been taught by him at the Academy in Glasgow, and it was Langmuir who had assisted in getting him a fellowship to study in London.

Grizel Langmuir's artistic genes also came from her mother, a watercolourist. Grizel had made her mark with oils – large, bold, sometimes brutal landscapes of some of the areas of Scotland which her father had treated in more decorative musical fashion.

She lived five or six miles along the coast. She either cycled into Auchendrennan, or walked. Sometimes she had company: those unmarried mature women or younger women art students who made up her circle, her 'Immortals' as she called them. (Her 'Immorals' as they were dubbed behind her back; but Aunt Nessie didn't tell me that.)

She was short, stocky, plain-looking, with a severe bun of greying hair. There was a touch of Queen Victoria about her, but dressed up in bohemian wear: long gypsy skirts or slacks, peasant blouses or Breton jumpers, chunky beads and bangles. She had an open face with, whenever I saw her, an agreeable expression on it. Like Bone she had alert querying eyes which had a way of holding you all the time she was speaking to you; and, when she looked away, you felt somehow disappointed, that she couldn't go on talking just to *you*.

I picked up an empty cigarette packet.

Abdulla No 37.

'What's that, Neil?'

'It must be Mr Maitland's.'

Bone grimaced. 'If it's a Wills', it's okay. Passing Clouds. Smoked them myself once.'

'Did you smoke these?'

'Abdulla's? No. Strictly for the professionals.'

'Mr Maitland?'

'Just for when he feels he needs something stronger.'

I slipped the carton into my pocket when Bone wasn't looking. Another souvenir.

★

Maitland was standing in one of the side-alleys from the beach as I hurried along Yett Street, to get to Slezer's Wark for two o'clock.

I halted without waiting for him to ask me to.

The expression on his face was hurt and hard.

'I'm not sure this is the best use of everyone's talents.'

I stared at him.

'Mr Bone's. Euan's,' he said. 'Or yours.'

'What isn't?' I asked him.

'The Lantern Bearers'.'

'But I *want* to.'

'His forte, I feel, is for – well, chamber works, but larger scale.'

113

'His songs,' I said, 'are famous.'

'School choirs, I fear, don't enthuse the critics a great deal.'

'Solo songs too.'

'Perhaps they're distracting him? From his other work – the more substantial things?'

I shook my head. That seemed to nettle him.

'I think,' he said, 'I'm in a better position to judge than you.'

But Bone himself had told me how enthusiastic their friends were with what they'd heard played to them of The Lantern Bearers. He'd let me know that Maitland was pleased by their reaction, and proud.

What had brought about this change of heart?

'I'll mention it again to Euan,' he said. 'Mr Bone. It's for his own good. And for yours too, my boy.'

★

A journalist was coming to interview Bone, but not to the house.

'Never again, Neil. Not after the last time.'

We finished work at 3.45, on the dot. Then Bone got up and left.

'Mrs Faichnie is to bring in tea just as usual. Sorry about this. See you tomorrow, Neil.'

Mrs Faichnie hadn't appeared by the time the downstairs telephone started to ring.

It went on ringing. No one came to answer it, either Mrs Faichnie or Maitland.

I moved to the door.

If I answered, I'd be showing my usefulness. If I didn't answer, they'd think I was completely unconcerned.

There wasn't time for debate.

I picked up the receiver.

A man's voice started to speak.

'Well, I can always tell when it's your other half.' He impersonated the Maitland telephone manner. ' "Slezer's Wark." "Who is this calling?" So, by a brilliant process of deduction …'

Then silence.

I asked, 'Who shall I say is calling?'

Immediately the receiver went down at the other end, and I was left listening to the abrupt hollowness of an empty line.

I turned round. Maitland was standing by the music room door.

'Someone rang,' I said.

'Who?'

'I don't know.'

'Who did they want?'

'Mr Bone.'

'Oh. Well, what did they say?'

'He just said – he knew it wasn't you.'

'He phoned up to say that?'

'I don't know why he was phoning.'

'What sort of voice?'

'Younger than – '

'Oh, everyone's younger than me.'

' – than Mr Bone.'

'I see. Peter Pan, was it?'

'I'm sorry – ?'

'Scottish? English?'

'I wasn't really – '

'Or foreign?'

'It might have been.' I couldn't actually recall. 'Not Scottish or English. But an *English*-speaker.'

'And you took it on yourself to answer the phone? Our phone?'

'There wasn't anyone here.'

'Don't be ridiculous. D'you think we'd leave you alone in the house?'

'I don't …'

There was an unpleasant imputation, I realised. I was piqued – and suddenly on the offensive.

I spoke, without giving myself adequate time to consider.

'Australian,' I said. 'Maybe.'

'What?'

'Somewhere like that. I can't …'

I couldn't bring back to mind what sort of accent it had been; I had been listening only to the sense. But now I was repaying Maitland for his insult. Saying 'Australian' changed the focus of his displeasure entirely.

Maitland's eyes narrowed at me.

'Are you sure?'

I might have made a show of racking my brain, trying to remember. But instead I smiled boldly back at him, and I didn't say anything.

115

'Shouldn't you be getting back now? I mean, won't your aunt be wondering …?'

I made for the front door. I could hear Maitland, a deep and heartfelt exhalation of pain that carried to me from where he was still standing – rooted to the spot – on the threshold of the music room.

★

I had just finished closing Aunt Nessie's front gate, still thinking of Maitland and the phone call, when Mr McLuskie appeared from next door. He preferred to use a gap between the yellow privet and copper beech hedges for entry.

His procedure didn't vary. He would address Aunt Nessie, not me.

'How's the lad getting on with the book?'

He would stand on one leg, with the other hitched up and his foot resting on the edge of a tub or the wheel of the wheelbarrow. He would lay his arm on the raised leg and bend forward, smiling into Aunt Nessie's face to ingratiate himself.

His proximity flummoxed her. Out would come the handkerchief from her cardigan cuff, so that she could dab at the film of perspiration on her brow and chin.

Today was no different.

'I'm sure you look after him very well, Miss Smeaton. He's a lucky fellow, he certainly is that.'

Aunt Nessie cranked out a smile. Her glazed eyes looked over in my direction, silently imploring.

I did my white knight good deed for the day, and came across to interrupt them.

'That's right,' she said, 'it's Neil's tea-time now.'

Mr McLuskie's smile for me was less warm.

'Doesn't know he's born, this one, I expect!'

Back in her own kitchen and composed again, Aunt Nessie was maintaining the pretence that there hadn't been anything wrong, she hadn't needed to be rescued. Standing at the sink she kept catching her eye in the little mirror nailed to the wall, taking furtive glances at herself.

I had noticed that she would primp herself even before she went out with the washing or to the dustbin. Just in case she was accosted. Unwittingly I was allowing her neighbour to be more intrusive, and Robert

116

Louis Stevenson had a hand in that. To begin with, her neighbour's attention might have flattered her, amused her; now his persistence was starting to alarm her, and souring that casual unserious enjoyment.

'Let's treat ourselves, Neil.' She opened the door of her cold cupboard. 'I was keeping the smoked salmon ends for my ladies. But I think we deserve our reward, don't you?'

Part Three

19

And then it happened, mid-way through the second half of my Galloway summer.

Standing at the piano one afternoon singing phrases after Bone, with Mrs Faichnie somewhere close by waiting to start preparations for tea, my voice ruptured.

My hand immediately flew to my throat.

Bone stopped playing and looked up at me with horror at the shock of the sound. Then his expression turned to irritation.

'Concentrate, Neil, will you?'

He started again – his fingers slid clumsily on the keys – but the same thing happened. A croak, a growl.

'*Again!*'

This time the piano keys were stabbed right into the wood. But for the third time my voice came out ragged and torn.

Bone leaped up from the stool. He crossed over to the window, leaned his brow against the glass, and stared outside. He didn't speak, or couldn't speak.

Over the bay clouds went cantering in a sunny optimistic sky. But that had nothing whatsoever to do with what was taking place here, inside the room.

The silence expanded on all sides of me. Not a sound was audible – even Mrs Faichnie's movements – nothing except the hard bundle of breath wheezing inside my chest.

I perched on the arm of a chair.

Bone was talking. At last. Speaking against the welter of thoughts in my head. He was wanting to test my voice again. But really, I knew, it was too late. What had occurred might very well occur a fourth time, and in that case for the fifth and sixth times and so on, even with the best will in the world that it shouldn't.

It was the dreaded break.

My voice was dropping.

Why *now*? I had come along to Slezer's Wark this afternoon as I always did, in happy spirits, to enjoy a manner of life I was becoming comfortable with, which excused all the petty tedium and mediocrity that was to be found in the rest of the town.

How could I disguise the crack? *Would* I be able to conceal it?

I already knew the answer.

I hauled myself to my feet.

Bone's face when I looked at it was older than only several moments ago, thinner and paler, with a greenish tinge. I stared at the bewilderment in his eyes, the twist to his mouth. His shoulders and arms were clenched.

He lowered himself on to the stool.

He was angry, I could see that quite well. At the same time he was completely at the mercy of circumstances.

He slammed down the keyboard lid. The strings in the case echoed eerily for miles. Then silence.

I stood where I was, I didn't dare to move.

I watched Bone sit shaking his head. At what had happened. At his own melodramatic reaction to the event, as if he couldn't define his responses any better to himself than some B-movie actor.

After that Bone's trust went, as did my confidence. We struggled on for a couple of days, but on both occasions my voice buckled. Bone waited at the keyboard, making a show of grudging patience, cracking the joints of his fingers.

'All right, Neil, we'll just have to leave it. It's not going to work like this, is it?'

I felt I had been possessed by some malevolent spirit determined to put an end to my pleasure, my charmed existence. Whenever I tried to steady my voice, to get a hold of myself, I would look over at the narrow side-window and focus my gaze on the clearest point in view, which was the tower of St Kentigern's Kirk. Somehow the difficulties became concentrated on that object, so that when I was back at Aunt Nessie's and forced over and over again to remember my shame in silence I saw the tower in my mind's eye. I saw it as realistically and *actually* as if I was looking at it at that very moment and not staring at the table cloth in the orange glow of the gas fire hissing on the wall.

'We'll just have to leave it. We can't go on.'

Bone accompanied me to the front door.

'Your time can be your own now.'

'I don't want it,' I said. 'I only want to – '

'What we *want*,' Bone said, 'and what we get ...'

He shrugged. That shrug meant, he surely didn't have to tell me, did he?

I understood that my voice had to change, and that the deepening was connected with the other physical awkwardnesses of the time. Arms and legs that wouldn't obey commands, the sticky leakings in my pyjama trousers, the darkening shadow above my upper lip. It wasn't a surprise to me, but it added to my self-consciousness.

Aunt Nessie looked aghast the first time my voice badly quavered in the house, and she started pulling at the beads round her neck so hard that I thought the string was going to snap. After that first shock she knew what to do, which was to ignore the matter. A pause would give the game away, but only for an instant: a double-take, a little stammer, no more than that, then Nessie Smeaton regained her equilibrium.

My voice might come back again.

If I *tried* to sing how I'd done then, earlier, maybe my voice would forget about the changes. I could coax it along, deal with a single phrase at a time; in that fashion, never mind it being slow work, the whole piece could be stitched together.

If I could just find some means of persuading Bone to give it another shot ...

It meant my getting up courage first. For that I refilled a schooner three times from the decanter of amontillado on top of Aunt Nessie's sideboard.

I heard the front door bang shut behind me before I realised I'd forgotten my key. Too bad. I made my way along the avenue tipsily, aware that I was leaning forward at an unlikely angle to somehow compensate for the keeling lampposts and trees.

I muddled down towards the old town, not bothered about whether I'd encounter Aunt Nessie's acquaintances or not. All I had to do was not look at them, and not reply if I was spoken to.

I kept my eyes fixed for my first glimpse of the white walls and the corbie-stanes on the gable-ends, the turret. Eyes peeled on the peel tower, I thought, and I started to laugh at my consummate wit.

I walked along Yett Street, taking care not to tread on any lines where the paving stones met one another, because if I did – if I did, I wasn't going to be able to go through with this.

I entered by the gates without stopping. But I slowed when I heard the gravel crunching under my feet. For a few moments doubts welled up … then the warm sherry consoled me, and I watched my shoes as my legs carried me forward, beneath the shade of the big cedar and out again, into the light, where I could be seen quite clearly from the house.

All I wanted was my voice back.

I didn't care about singing a tenor's part one day, and shaving once a week or twice a week.

I understood what mattered to me now. My priorities were all worked out.

Simply, to return.

I rang the front bell. It sounded far away inside the house. But the door was opened within seconds, as if my arrival had been anticipated, observed from one of the windows.

I found myself looking up at, not Mrs Faichnie, but Douglas Maitland.

His right hand was resting on his checked waistcoat, the fingers were fidgeting with the watch chain.

He bowed his head slightly to acknowledge me. A faint smile followed, for courtesy's sake.

He seemed in better humour than at our last encounter, following the telephone call.

Suddenly I couldn't remember what it was I meant to say.

'I'm afraid,' that bespoke voice above me announced, 'Euan – Mr Bone – has had to go away today.'

'Will he – will he – .' I cleared my throat, staring at the pattern of checks on his waistcoat. '… will he be back tomorrow, Mr Maitland?'

'I'm unsure about that. What his movements are going to be.' His tone was distant, but not cold. 'I can't really tell you, alas.'

'Shall I – if I telephone – ' I spoke quickly, before the crack could come back into my voice.

'I think – well, he'll probably write to you. Sorry you've had a fruitless journey.'

I don't know what caused me to do it, but where the drive started to veer away from the house, I returned to the high beech hedge.

124

I followed it for several more yards and then stopped. Maybe I just wanted a last sight of the garden. I reached into the hedge, tried prising the branches apart. I went up on tiptoe, craned forward to get a view through the leaves on the other side.

There he was. Bone. Sitting – half-lying – in a striped canvas deck-chair. He had a book in his hand but his head was thrown back, his eyes were closed. Behind him the sun was reflected, slivers and parings of sun, in the small-paned doors of the octagonal summerhouse. A wood pigeon was chortling overhead where I couldn't see, puffing itself up every time to reprise its tattoo of contentment.

I stared at him. At the man who was allegedly absent, but no more than fifteen yards from me.

That outsized head, the storm-whipped hair even though there was no wind today, the stubborn chin and the sensualist's mouth. In that posture of relaxed, uninhibited normality. The dragging seat of the deck-chair; the yellow, green, orange, brown stripes of the canvas.

Every small last detail –

Now Aunt Nessie could hear for herself why I wasn't going off to Slezer's Wark any more.

'For the meantime,' I said, inventing, and meaning to placate myself as well as Aunt Nessie.

'That seems a pity. A wee bit of a waste, doesn't it?'

I couldn't bring myself to nod agreement.

'Och well then,' she said, and from that I deduced she felt at a loss to know what to do with me, how she was going to keep me occupied and so distracted from unhappy thoughts about home.

I went into a brown mood, a sort of sensual depression which coincided with an extreme sensitivity to temperature on the surface of my skin. I alighted on a photograph of Bone in a newspaper, taken a few years before, and simultaneously I experienced urgent stirrings in my groin. The music started to play back inside my head; I felt again the warmth of his breath on the back of my neck, a sensation of locked sight and a tightening in my stomach as he pointed out to me something or other on a page of manuscript.

Aunt Nessie had come in to dust and vacuum my room. I saw her looking at the cover of the book Mr McLuskie had lent me.

125

'I haven't finished it,' I said.

'Are you enjoying it?'

'It's not a story. They're essays.'

She didn't pick the book up, but dusted around it.

'Are you going to finish it, d'you think?'

'I'm not sure.'

'It's up to you.'

She took her yellow duster up under the shade of my bedside lamp.

'Should I give it back to him?' I asked.

Aunt Nessie furrowed her brow, as if she was having to concentrate hard on the corner of the dressing-table she was dusting.

'I could give it back,' I said. 'He wouldn't know.'

'Well ... You could keep it a wee while longer, couldn't you? You never know, you might want to read a bit more, no?'

I nodded. That was easiest for me, I felt. Avoidance.

Momentarily Aunt Nessie's eyes returned to the book, to confirm its reprieve. Avoidance for both of us.

★

Slezer's Wark
Yett Street
Auchendrennan

Tel: 2137

19.viii.62

Dear Neil,

I don't really see how we can continue, do you? Tempora mutantur, but rotten timing all round, I'd say. We were making such good progress too.

Hope you enjoyed yourself and it wasn't too much like hard work.

I expect you'll be going back soon? Dear old Glescae toun. (I wonder.)

Good luck.

In haste.

Regards,

E.B.

Wavy lines were scoring Aunt Nessie's brow. Now she understood why.

She folded the letter and returned it to its envelope. She handed the envelope back to me.

'Well, that's that then.'

We were standing in the middle of the hall. Neither of us had the excuse of a distraction. I had closed my bedroom door; the mirror on the coat stand was just out of Aunt Nessie's range of vision.

'Should I go back home?' I asked in my treacherously unstable voice. 'Back to Glasgow?'

Aunt Nessie's reply was instantaneous.

'No. No, not yet.'

She smiled at me, a commiserating smile with some genuine pity in it.

'This – this is your home for just now. Until the summer goes.'

I nodded, feeling it was a dismal prospect. Two more weeks of Auchendrennan left.

Along the Saut Wynd, 'Salt Lane'. Touch the rusty capstan on the harbour side. Turn on my heels and back into Fishmercat. Up Gallowgait at a run. Past the Dreadnought Hotel. Onwards and up, by any of the back ways. Into the chill that fell from the shadow of Bailie Smee's Mausoleum. Then my first sight of the Celtic Cross, with its 'jougs' – the iron collar – for wrong-doers attached. And, beyond, the unassailable greystone villas in their monkey puzzle-tree gardens.

Why now?

My eyes kept returning, from wherever I happened to be, to the tower of St Kentigern's Kirk.

Why now? And for how long?

Aunt Nessie would dutifully go off to her kirk, St John's and St James's, every Sunday morning, with my sceptical self in tow. She was a stalwart of the Woman's Guild, but I'd suspected that her loyalty was on social not spiritual grounds. Aunt Nessie and I invariably returned from church in a shower of rain; two or three times we'd been quite drookit indeed, so that we'd had to dry off our good clothes in front of the fire after changing into others, as of course we always did anyway. I didn't know what point God was wanting to make with the drenching – perhaps He was trying to test our faith? Metaphysical speculation wasn't Aunt Nessie's way, however, and she only ever remarked on the inconvenience, not on the uncanny coincidence.

Was it the same divine mischief-making that was also responsible for the damage being inflicted on my voice?

Why *now*? And for how long?

20

I waited for Bone to write to me again, or to phone.

I waited. I didn't hear, though.

I felt he would want to get back to The Lantern Bearers, that he'd take a risk with my voice.

But every time the phone rang at Skerryvore, it was for Aunt Nessie, not for me. The only mail I received amounted to a couple of milk-and-water letters, one from my mother and one from my father, sent out of bleak duty and surely telling me nothing of what had been going on in my absence.

From one day to the next the roses in the front beds were losing their splendour. No longer ripe and voluptuous as I remembered them, they hung their heads, as if dispirited themselves that they couldn't live up to their reputation for glorious vulgarity. Even blowsiness requires continual energy, and they just didn't have it in them any more.

When I looked, everything in the garden – except the dahlias – appeared to be on the wane. The colours were faded, the flowerheads sagged and were shedding their petals, nothing stood as tall as it used to. All that was left was a running down and soughing away.

' – he's auditioning them. Like with your Neil.'

I paused with my hand on the handle of my bedroom door.

I recognised Jean Shearer's voice.

In the sitting-room tea cups clinked back into their saucers.

' – the best Bone could manage anyhow.'

' – won't be as good as Neil.'

Marjorie, Nan.

' – has to do something, mind.'

' – ungrateful, though.'

' – just the way of it, I suppose.'

Tea-spoons chimed on the china.

' – and beggars can't be choosers, Nessie.'

Could it have been that I'd been using my voice too much?

But what was the alternative: that I shouldn't have sung, and not had my time at Slezer's Wark, which was to have a bearing on the rest of my life?

Losing my voice was part of the deal – to have played a role in creating something which had given him so much pride.

My own feelings, then and now, didn't even matter. The music had been, and would be, everything.

I would throw my voice – walking along a back street (but not one of the avenues) – to surprise it, and I would listen for the old voice. Sometimes it was there and sometimes it wasn't. When it was there I would run along the pavement, jumping from stone to stone and not treading on the lines where they joined, because if I did I was bound to lose it again. But I always overstepped the mark, and my foot grazed a line, and the next time I flung my voice ahead of me, the old voice contained inside that one had gone, and I was left with this raw flayed substitute.

I was unable to keep away from Yett Street. And that was how I saw my replacement arriving, with some manuscript pages untidily stuffed under one arm.

But my shock was double what it might have been.

I had been superseded by a boy with vivid red hair, the ringleader of the street gang which had jeered at me as I hurried past them, wolf-whistling me down the hilly streets.

I was there the next afternoon, come half-past four, when he left the house.

On his way out he picked up some gravel chips from the driveway and took aim with them at a tom cat. The cat sprang into the air, then vanished beneath a parked car.

The boy dropped the manuscript pages he was carrying, they scattered on the road. He roughly snatched them up, bundling them in a boorie – every which way – beneath his arm.

For something to do, and because it was one of those days when Aunt Nessie would wheeze past me into the bathroom with her Woman's Problem and stay locked inside for twenty minutes at a time with the taps running to prevent me hearing, I had gone out.

130

All the way round Carntyre Point, to the rocks, to where the pools of water collected.

They were on the beach, with their backs turned to me. Bone and the red-haired boy.

Bone's hand tapped the boy's shoulder to indicate that he should stop and look at something embedded in the wet sand. My substitute paused, turned back, examined whatever was being pointed out to him. Then he began to dig at the object with the heel of his plimsoll. Bone had to apply his hand again, to the arm this time, to stop him. The boy looked up. Bone was shaking his head. No, no, this wasn't supposed to happen.

They moved off together. I stood watching them both. I felt little charity for Bone, even when I saw him being so put out. The boy was no adequate replacement for me, and I smiled to know it. Just because his voice hadn't broken, that was no guarantee of suitability.

I smiled coldly after the pair of them.

The boy was kicking dry sand at his shadow. Bone glanced at him, then lowered his head, averting his eyes. He must have continued talking because he was waving his explaining hand as he used to do with me, to highlight some musical point he wanted to make, but the boy's attention was all for his own slanting shadow on the sand. Their legs didn't move in tandem, the way I used to like mine to do with Bone's, synchronising; they were out of rhythm, which I would never have allowed, and they stayed that way.

I felt my smile freezing over my top gum.

When the two figures were too small to observe in any detail, my eyes returned to the rock pools. I pictured the boy's method of studying the specimens Bone had found for him: prising them out of their shells or letting them slap around the bare rock or pulling at their fronds.

I hoped and hoped the boy's end would come soon, and that Bone would rue the day he had brought him to Slezer's Wark. It was what they both deserved, for letting the memory of his predecessor lapse so easily. They shouldn't be left to get away with it, and suddenly I had a premonition – with a terrible little surge of certainty, with a stabbing smug joy – that they neither of them would.

131

21

I counted the days left on the calendar on the kitchen wall. I didn't know where I wanted to be. If not here in Auchendrennan, then not back in Glasgow either.

Aunt Nessie was afraid I'd find myself at a loose end, so she invented jobs for me to do. I had to pretend that I was quite content otherwise to be out and about, exercising my legs, filling my lungs with sea air to last me through an autumn and winter back in the smoky city.

I hung about Yett Street in the afternoons, but I didn't catch a sight of my replacement on his way to or from Slezer's Wark. Maybe Bone had changed his working hours? I switched to the mornings instead. And when I didn't see the boy in the mornings, I tried to take as much time out of the day as possible to cover that quarter of the town.

When it rained, I took shelter in doorways, and – if the houseowners got restless – under the tree of broadest branches I could see.

Isla passed me once or twice on her bicycle, too afraid to stop now.

Aunt Nessie told me I was 'looking the better' for the hours I spent out of doors, but I didn't say that I felt no better inside.

An emptiness had replaced those earlier sentiments of shame and sorrow and also anger. It seemed to me that far longer than nine or ten days separated me from the boy I'd been then.

Mrs Faichnie was approaching along North Street. In the middle the street narrowed to one pavement. We couldn't avoid one another.

She'd seen me, and was twisting her mouth in anticipation.

I stopped a few feet in front of her. I thought she was going to carry on walking, but at the very last moment she seemed to take pity on me.

'I haven't been,' I said.

'No.'

'I'm not singing now.'

My voice was the evidence of that.

'Well, you can start to enjoy yourself a bit more.'

'But – but I did. I did enjoy myself.'

'I'm afraid I don't understand it.'

About my having enjoyed myself? – about the loss of my voice? I didn't know which she was talking about.

She hitched her basket up on to her arm.

'Well, their dinner won't get itself, I suppose.'

I stepped back, to let her pass.

'My regards to Miss Smeaton,' she said.

Then I saw the red-haired boy back up on the wall, with his gang, two afternoons in succession.

I went back the second time to check, and heard them laughing at me again, for my impudence in returning to the spot.

I listened to make out his voice. It was still unbroken. He yelled over, 'You can have him back again, it's rubbish.'

The others started chanting. 'Rubbish, rubbish, rubbish!'

What was? The music?

'It's bollocks.'

'Bollocks, bollocks, bollocks!'

But it was my music. Mine and Bone's.

I dropped a look over my shoulder which I meant to be withering, recalling one I'd received from Bone. Maybe I was too convincing. Their laughter trailed away menacingly.

'Fairy!' one of them called after me.

'Pansy!'

Then I started to run. Off and away, hell for leather.

Bone still went swimming. But he swam alone.

I sat high up in the dunes to watch. I hadn't realised how often he changed stroke. Breaststroke, fast crawl, on to his back, side-paddle, a spurt of butterfly. He didn't stick at one for longer than twenty or thirty seconds. As a result his swimming looked frantic, viewed from here. When I'd been swimming with him, though, I had only thought how strong and even his arm thrusts and leg kicks were.

I had a perfect *right* to be at Yett Street.

It had felt truer to me, to the person I really was, than Aunt Nessie's bungalow did.

Did they really think they could keep me away from the place?

One evening I stayed out late.
I took with me the torch I'd bought with the ten-shilling note.
I shone a track across the rocks, leading to the sea wall of the garden.
When I got there, the old wooden gate wasn't locked.
I lifted the latch, pushed gently against the wood. I stepped forward.
I switched off the torch. I stood looking in.
Now I could make-believe the garden was mine. They wouldn't be able to see me from inside the house, from their lit rooms.
Whatever I wished …
I could dance across the lawn. I could pick whichever flowers I wanted to. I could piss on a flowerbed. I could say 'shit!' and even 'fuck!' right out loud.
I imagined that, now, I needn't ever leave.
They were keeping behind their windows. Sometimes a head or a back came into view, then passed out of the frame. And it was all by my command.
If I clicked my fingers, the lights would go off, one by one. At another click the wind might blow up, and a squall would beat against those harled walls. If I clicked my fingers again – I was back at Skerryvore, awake in my bed, lying remembering: remembering layer under layer under layer of my memories.

★

Aunt Nessie was having another hot flush.
Or so I thought when I walked in next day for lunch, back with her messages from the shops.
She was fussing about, at different points of the kitchen. Keeping busy, keeping busy.
Her eyes briefly made contact with mine.
The egg pot was on top of the cooker, but she didn't light the gas.
'I thought you could take that book back,' she said. 'Before you eat.'
'Yes. All right. I haven't managed to fin– '
'And if you do, we don't need to give it another thought.'
She reached for the box of matches.
'You nip round now. And you'll be back before your egg's ready.'

'What if he speaks to me?'

She opened the box, gave the matches inside a good shake.

'He won't.'

Mr McLuskie's gate creaked when I let myself in.

I saw a shape standing behind the net curtains in one of the front rooms.

I rang the doorbell and waited.

There was no reply. He must have heard the chimes, though.

I thought I could push the book through the letterbox. But it might fall with its covers splayed, and the pages would crease. So instead I left the book propped up next to the front door; the vestibule arch gave it some cover from the sun.

From behind the hedge, as I was walking back along the pavement to Skerryvore, I heard his front door lock turning. The book was being retrieved already. Sixpence he'd paid for it: sixpence wasted and sluiced down the drain for nothing.

★

I went back to Yett Street in the afternoon.

Maitland walked out of one of the side-alleys to the beach and blocked my path.

'What brings you this way again?'

I didn't know what to say to him.

'Have you told your aunt where you go?'

I spoke in my new voice. 'No.'

Maitland took a couple of steps back. 'No, I thought not.'

'But she can guess,' I said. I couldn't hold myself back now. 'She knows plenty of things. I don't have to say. She knows all right.'

Maitland opened his mouth, shaped some words, but didn't speak them straightaway.

He turned to look behind him, along the road. What I'd said seemed to have him ruffled.

He turned round again.

'Look – just get away from here, will you?'

'What?'

'I think you heard me.'

'It's a public road.'

'From the road. From Auchendrennan. Just clear off.'

I was too taken aback to reply at once.

'You won't believe me, but I'm thinking of what's best.'

'For *you*?'

'No. Best for you. Just do what I say, please.'

Now I was too indignant to speak.

'Go back home to your friends, Neil Pritchard. Just forget this place.'

'You *want* me to go?' My old squeaky voice sounded through the new deeper one.

'Forget this place and forget us. It's over.'

'It's *not* over.'

'What else is there?'

'It isn't time to go back,' I shouted over the boy's voice.

'Okay, pipe down.'

'It's still summer.'

'Keep it a good memory.'

'It's not now, though,' I said.

'Get away, then. You'll forget the bad parts.'

I was still living them, the bad parts. Why couldn't he see that?

'It's got nothing to do with you,' I heard myself telling him. 'It's none of your business.'

'It *is* my business. If you suffer for it.'

What did he mean? 'Suffer for it'? Wasn't that precisely what I was doing?

'Then you'll wish you'd listened to me,' he went on, 'paid me heed.'

I spun round on my heels and quickly walked away from him. I was still seeing his alarmed eyes with the fretwork of crow's feet around them. But it was useless, trying to argue with him about any of this.

He called after me.

'Don't turn your back on me, Neil. That doesn't solve anything.'

He raised his voice.

'Neil, d'you hear me – ?'

It wasn't really a question, was it?

I was shaking, and sick to the pit of my flip-over stomach.

But I wasn't going to give any answer except this one, to keep on walking away from him. Along Yett Street, back towards the old town. Picking up speed; faster now, breaking into a run.

22

Maitland left that evening (according to Mrs Faichnie, who put it about on the grapevine), to give some solo recitals, in Birmingham and Manchester.

I continued to watch close by the house so that I could chart Bone's movements.

Sometimes he used the car, but just as often he didn't.

I followed him about Auchendrennan without ever calling out and addressing him. I wanted him to know I was there, so I allowed him to see me. I stood outside shops he went into, so that he could look back when he was inside and notice me waiting on the pavement. I trailed him doggedly on his constitutionals; I maintained an even distance between us, and he would turn his head every so often and catch me there in the corner of his eye.

Notwithstanding Maitland's warnings, I stood about Yett Street, to see any arrivals and departures. I went down to the beach, in case Bone was using the front gate in the wall, and where I knew I'd be visible from the windows of the music room and – even more obvious – from the upstairs drawing-room.

One evening when Aunt Nessie was out I called on her phone. When Bone answered I said nothing into the mouthpiece but just listened to his voice, asking who this was please ... Until he replaced the receiver and I was left with the bbrr-r-r-r of an open line stuttering in my ear.

Twice I walked a neighbour's spaniel, which allowed me to get out and watch Slezer's Wark when the windows were lit. On the second night there were cars parked outside which I didn't recognise, and figures moving about in the rooms who were similarly unfamiliar to me: younger men, but a few women too, the confident sort of female who contrives to live life on her own terms.

Something, I felt, was waiting to happen.

Beyond our own small activities there was a silence without end. Inside the hills, in the deeps of the sea, amorphous in the sky.

We drove Dinky cars, and the trains that came in and out of Auchendrennan were Hornby-Dublo, and the people strode about by clever clockwork, and our Solway market-town was on the very far edge of a continent, on its outermost ring. I knew all that. But even so, it was as if the elements themselves were holding their breath.

I continued to follow Bone about the streets. I watched him from high points on the dunes when he went walking across the beach. From the road I always had the black rocks in my sights.

I didn't attempt to conceal myself. That wasn't the point at all. I saw him looking; sometimes he turned right round, if only for a second or two, to confirm his suspicions.

He had to finish the piece, The Lantern Bearers, didn't he understand that? He had to keep faith with it, and so honour justice for us both. He owed it to his own talent, and I wanted him to know that – however unfairly he had treated me – I was still fast and endlessly loyal in his service.

I walked about Upper Craigs. I watched the lights come on in the villas.

One night I stayed out so late that I watched the houses go dark again at bedtime.

When I got back to Skerryvore, only the table-lamp in the hall was lit. I knocked over the milk-bottle on the back step. I saw a light go on in Aunt Nessie's bedroom as I passed through the hall; then it was pointedly switched off again.

And so I should just forget? How *could* I forget?

I turned the centre light on in my own room. I kicked off my shoes. One of them hit the wall and left a mark on the paper. Still wearing my clothes I dropped on to the bed, on my back, crumpling the soft candlewick. The springs complained.

I pushed my hand down into my trousers, inside my underpants. My knob felt like a rosebud, and I tugged at it. I yanked, but nothing happened.

I learned from Aunt Nessie in the morning, it had been arranged that I should go back to Glasgow on Saturday.

'Behind my back?'

'What's that?'

'You talked to my parents? You asked them?'

'I feel … well, it's been a fair long time.'

138

'You want to get rid of me, Aunt Nessie?'

'It's almost time anyway. You've less to do now. You must be missing the big city. Auchendrennan – I don't think this place has got anything more to give you, Neil.'

'Till Tuesday?'

'No, Neil. I'm sorry.'

23

The front door of Slezer's Wark was standing open.

I rang the bell.

Then I knocked.

I called inside.

I waited for the sound of Mrs Faichnie's feet on the hall tiles.

A cello case was propped against a chair. The lid of the case carried Maitland's initials. He must have come back.

I called again.

'Mr Bone?'

I waited. From upstairs I thought I heard a voice. Voices. A door opening, closing.

But no footsteps.

I stepped into the hall, past the oak door. Past the passageway to the cloakroom.

I looked up the stairwell. The voices sounded far away, perhaps up on the floor where the bedrooms were.

I walked on.

I saw ahead into the music room.

I crossed over and went in.

My stomach was tied in a knot. My breath came in short, tight bursts. I'd thought I wouldn't ever be here again. In Slezer's Wark, the house with the crazy name. Standing in the music room.

I stared across at the piano, the manuscripts chest, the lectern where I used to stand. The paintings, by Cadell and Peploe; the Venetian mirror that wasn't.

I looked behind me.

Still no Mrs Faichnie. I didn't smell her soapy, Heather Tweed presence, so falsely sweet.

I walked forward to the piano.

The music board was empty.

I passed behind the stool. I went to the third drawer of the manuscripts cabinet, which was where Bone had always gone to fetch his Lantern Bearers' sheets.

I looked inside. I searched beneath what was on top. It was the fourth or fifth item I came to, held together by a brass clip. A familiar mess of pencil marks on the printed staves.

I turned to the final pages. The last two of all were new, but included a number of heavy scorings-out.

I didn't *plan* to take it.

An instinct made me do it.

I pushed the drawer shut.

Seconds later I was at the door of the room. Then I was out in the hall. The same silence as before.

I tiptoed down the hall. No floorboard creaks to give me away.

I wasn't trusting my luck to hold, though. It seemed so easy. Too easy.

I didn't stop, I didn't give myself a chance to think about what I was doing.

I ran past the front door, down the steps. I sprinted across the gravel, to the cover of the trees. I pushed the manuscript pages up under my pullover, and tucked the pullover into the waistband of my trousers.

I ran all the way to Aunt Nessie's.

My heart was up in my throat.

(I wasn't stealing, I kept telling myself, I was borrowing back.)

Along the avenues. In league with the protective hedges. Privet, beech, laurel, seaside holly.

(I needed to have the manuscript itself, to fathom what the past few weeks had been about.)

Round the corner into Colquhoun. By the dog's-leg into the twenty yards of lane with the high creosote fence. Out again into Hauselock.

Counting the roofs. Three, four, five, until I saw the douce grey slate tiles of Skerryvore.

In my bedroom that night I positioned the chair up hard against the door, jamming the back under the handle.

Then I fetched the manuscript from beneath the bed.

I stayed up until three o'clock, copying out the music in blue ballpoint and precisely setting the words beneath the notation just as Bone had done. There were points where he repeated himself, and I became confused, but I copied those out too: every jot and tittle. In a few places he'd got the words wrong, or misplaced the order; I wanted my copy to be utterly faithful, like a carbon, and I made no changes.

I ran my fingertips over his pencil marks. I felt the impressions he'd made on the page when he'd been working quickly and dashing down the notes. I held the pages up to the light, the ones where he'd rubbed out with an eraser, and I tried to decipher what had been beneath and considered better of.

Eighty per cent or more was material I had sung for Bone. The remainder was an attempt to match his earlier inspiration, but I guessed that it had been laboured over.

I heard Aunt Nessie up sometime after two o'clock, shuffling through in her slippers to the bathroom. She seemed to slow, and I realised she would be able to see a chink of light beneath my door – and perhaps the outline of the chair's legs. She paused again on her way back; there was half a minute of silence before she carried on through to bed.

★

Mrs Faichnie wasn't bothered who heard her. She had done her bounden and beholden bit, and a fat lot of thanks she'd got from the one who should've appreciated it most: given what Douglas Maitland Esquire had to lose if she should choose to open her mouth and blab.

She wasn't blabbing quite yet. But she had no mind to be cautious either. She decided that the front of The Girnel tea-rooms was as good as anywhere to begin, with her two cronies from the Woman's Guild.

Nelly McCaig immediately afterwards told Jean Shearer, who came round to Skerryvore to tell Aunt Nessie. They stood with their tea in the kitchen, Melrose's, as the best fresh gossip required.

I told myself I didn't want to hear, not just then.

I heard some months later, and I recognised the truth of it at once. But would anything have been altered if I'd known at the time, if I'd just brazenly eavesdropped at the door to Jean Shearer's first eager telling?

According to Mrs Faichnie Bone hadn't accused Maitland of taking the manuscript he found himself looking for. 'The Lantern Something-or-other'. Or of 'mislaying' it.

But Maitland accused Bone of presuming he had. He said Bone wouldn't ask him straight-out because he must've thought he'd be lied to.

142

Is that what you think of me? Maitland went on repeating. And then he'd sworn, bad swearing at that, the worst.

Well, *he* didn't know how it could've happened, Bone said back.

And Maitland's response was, You've got your list of suspects, I'll bet. Or should that be in the singular?

Later Maitland came into Mrs Faichnie's kitchen, tanked up on sherries and gins, and he started insinuating her fingerprints were all over the business. She was the one paid to do the tidying up, who knew where everything went. So who else could possibly –

At that Mrs Faichnie used the tongue in her head, and how.

When he'd gone – sent packing from the kitchen – she had tears in her eyes, now she didn't mind admitting it. She took off her housecoat right there and then, hung it up on the pantry door, and went for her mac. In the hall she heard the two of them upstairs, an altercation, a real ding-dong. A thud, a sound like a chair falling over. And something smashing. Maitland bawling. Bone shouting over him, pleading with him to calm down – please calm down, Douglas – and Maitland telling him to keep his hands to himself.

A right stooshie.

Mrs Faichnie let the front door slam shut behind her. Even from the steps she could hear them still going at it.

★

I waited until Aunt Nessie was outside in the front garden. Then I pushed the manuscript up inside my pullover, and left the house by the kitchen door.

I had no idea how I was going to return the pages.

In Souter's Vennel a stone skittered between my feet, thrown from behind. Another followed. A third got me in the small of my back.

'Nancy boy!'

'What's under your jumper?'

'Looks like he's up the spout!'

'Poof!'

Sticks and stones.

I raced for the way out into Wellgait. Dashing past them, bumping against their padded hips, I noticed a couple of Aunt Nessie's friends. I hadn't time to apologise, and I left them with their mouths flapping open.

143

Aunt Nessie would give me a proper talking-to when she found out; I couldn't say to her that it was my rudeness which had saved my skin.

On Tanhouse Brae, round the corner from the Dreadnought Hotel, I stopped.

Maitland's Facel convertible was parked across the road, outside a tobacconist's shop.

I stared at the car.

In my future memories I'm standing staring at the white and blue car, which has its hood folded down. I'm not planning anything, just as I didn't intend to take the manuscript. But I know what to do now.

I cross the road. I look into the car. I push the button on the glove compartment lid. I pull the rolled pages of the original from under my jumper, and I stuff them into the compartment's hold. I try to close the lid again, but I can't get the button to click shut. I apply more pressure, and then the button does engage.

I hear the bell ringing on the tobacconist's door. I dive into the doorway of Murray's ironmonger's next to it.

I watch from behind the hanging brooms.

It's not Maitland who appears, walking to the kerb. It's Bone. Bone alone.

He's bought a box of cigars.

He's going to leave the box on the front passenger seat, perhaps before he goes off to another shop. But he thinks better of that and leans into the car, presses the button of the glove compartment.

Like me he's unused to the lock, and has to press again.

He's about to stash his purchase inside when he recognises something written on the top page of manuscript paper. He pulls out the roll of pages. He quickly looks through what's there.

He raises his head, and stands looking in the direction the Facel is facing, which is the way back to Yett Street. He is perfectly still for several moments. He is going to return the manuscript to the glove compartment, but instead he makes a tube of the pages and places it in his jacket pocket.

If he meant to go anywhere else, he's forgotten. He walks round to the driver's door, opens it and slides down on to the seat. He slams the door shut.

He sits for three or four minutes. He puts his elbow up on the sill, taps his hand on the outside of the door. A slow tattoo.

Is he waiting for someone?

No, because nobody comes.

He pulls the manuscript out of his pocket. He seems to be weighing it in his left hand: calculating the significance of this discovery, assessing the implications.

When he starts the engine, he presses too hard down on the accelerator, because he's unfamiliar with the choreography of the pedals.

The engine revs. Bone pulls too sharply on the wheel and the car shoots out into the road.

I'm recalling the first day I saw Bone, and Maitland, and their two friends, from the steps of St John's and St James's. It was only six and a half weeks ago, but it could have been six and a half months, or longer.

When I remember to look again, the Facel has gone.

24

Aunt Nessie glanced over at the clock.

'You're not going to be late back again?'

'I don't know.'

'Only, you'll have to get your milky drink. It's bad for you last thing. You shouldn't go right to bed on a – '

'But it's summer. I don't – ' My voice wobbled again. ' – need a milky drink.'

'You didn't mind before.'

Maybe the hot Ovaltine had taken a toll of my vocal chords. Why not? Every channel of possibility had to be explored.

'Well, I'll wait up.'

'You don't need to,' I said.

'Folk roundabout here don't stay out late. Maybe your parents let you …'

She stopped herself from saying more.

'I'll be all right,' I told her.

Aunt Nessie nodded, not very positively. She didn't approve, but I'd had a rough ride. She could surely hear all the disappointment stored up in my sandpaper voice.

I saw Bone leaving the Tulliebardine Hotel. He was with Grizel Langmuir and another woman. They stood for a while in front of the lit vestibule talking to an older couple, who'd recognised them. The couple moved off, and Bone and the other two walked away in the opposite direction; the second woman was laughing merrily, and her companions each held an arm.

Grizel Langmuir opened the door of her car. Bone got in first, into the back, and then the second woman fell inside and landed on top of him. More hilarity.

The car started up. But it turned left, not right, which would have taken it to Yett Street. At the fork it signalled right again, for Elcho Brae, the higher of the two coastal roads out of Auchendrennan.

No sign of Maitland.

It was half-past eleven.

I walked along Yett Street and reached the gateposts of Slezer's Wark. Only one room was lit, Maitland's bedroom.

In the darkness the white walls loomed eerily, icily. The stepped corbie-stanes on the roof looked like a giant's teethmarks, hungry bites gnawed out of the night sky.

★

Two weeks later, after her second and more dramatic showdown with Maitland and when I was no longer around to hear, Mrs Faichnie would carefully let slip that there had been another to-do between the two men.

Someone was being spoken about: a recent visitor, a young cellist or a violinist (Mrs Faichnie couldn't bring to mind which). Maitland was going on about the summer, and how awful it had been, and how they should have gone to Italy as he'd suggested they should and none of this would have happened.

'And *you* wouldn't have started drinking again,' Bone said.

'What else is there to do?'

'The other summers were okay.'

'*They* were ...'

(Maitland went on to use a word about Auchendrennan that began with an 'f', and she couldn't repeat it.)

'And bloody Robert Louis Stevenson.'

Bone told him he thought he was being 'rather selfish'. Maitland exploded at that. If it hadn't been for him getting Bone back on the straight and narrow, he'd done everything for Bone, made it possible for him to work again, get the success he was due ...

'And *you* haven't done too badly out of it either, career-wise.'

'You think that's why I did it?'

'Oh Douglas, Douglas – I didn't say that was the *reason* why you did it – '

'You're implying it, though.'

'We're getting a mite hysterical, I – '

'I'm "hysterical" now ...'

And so it went on. At intervals throughout the afternoon. Not quite hammer and tongs, because Maitland was the one always taking offence.

Bone tried to sweet-talk him out of it, but Maitland was resisting all those old terms of affection Mrs Faichnie had overheard them both using in the past.

Doors slammed. They were opened, and promptly banged shut again.

Nothing like that ever used to happen. The summer had brought it on.

Mrs Faichnie kept in the kitchen. She saw from the window as Bone got the Jensen out of the garage. He had a suitcase with him. He came back indoors for a hold-all, and several pairs of shoes, and his burberry. And his music-case. It looked as if he was planning to be away for a while. She wanted to ask him where he was going, but she was afraid to get involved.

She watched Bone drive off, noticed the last backwards-glance he gave over his shoulder, how he adjusted the wing-mirror as if he was trying to hold the house in it, so he wouldn't miss the sight of Maitland calling him back.

But Maitland didn't appear.

She'd found out next morning that Bone was being put up by Grizel Langmuir further down the coast.

Mrs Faichnie was jealous; she confessed as much. And possibly that made her more off-hand with Maitland, who was being very difficult as it was after his hangover and on his way to a second.

'What bloody business is this of yours? You're here to housekeep. I can see whose side *you're* on.'

'I don't take sides. I've got no feelings about anything, I'm only a housekeeper – '

'Oh, go hang, woman!'

'I'll ask you to remember to keep a civil tongue – .'

'I want the place to myself,' he told her. 'Come back when I tell you – '

He gave her her next week's wages.

' – and not before.'

★

Aunt Nessie had done my washing and ironing. She helped me start my packing.

She asked me if there was anything special I wanted to do for my last day.

I shrugged.

'Well, let me know, won't you?'

I hadn't looked at the music again. I couldn't bear to.

On my final afternoon in the house, I realised I couldn't take it with me.

I did what I did next with little more forethought than when I'd taken the manuscript and, later, replaced it.

I fetched a hammer from beneath the kitchen sink. I pulled back the carpet and underfelt in my bedroom. I tested the floorboards. I knew there was a loose one which I walked over every time I crossed the room.

I was able to angle it up at one end with the claws of the hammer, just far enough to slip my copy of the manuscript, bound with an elastic band, into the darkness beneath. I didn't hear the papers drop. It was as if they'd fallen into a bottomless black well. I smelt the sourness of dust and old time.

I eased the board back down and stamped on it. Then I replaced the underfelt and carpet. I forgot about the hammer, until Aunt Nessie came in with a freshly ironed shirt. I couldn't think what to say, why the hammer was here in my bedroom, but Aunt Nessie was in a mood to forgive.

'I'll take that back to the kitchen,' she said, and picked it up. She held the hammer at arm's length as if she was frightened of its lethal potential, as if she was handling forensic evidence.

And it was as simple a matter as that.

On my last evening Aunt Nessie had her friends in, and I was to join them.

When the others were making their way through to the dining-room I stayed behind in the sitting-room and took a long swig from the sherry decanter.

At the table, while we tackled the boiled ham, I thought I was being outstandingly witty. There were a few smiles to begin with, but no laughter followed as I opined on the life of the town. I told them just what I thought about the shopkeepers, and the tawdry stock they sold, the people with charge-accounts and put-you-down accents who wriggled out of paying; I didn't spare the church minister, the tedium of his sermons, the out-of-tune voices in the elderly choir. Our nosy neighbours on Hauselock Avenue …

'Thank you, Neil,' Aunt Nessie broke in. 'We'll excuse you now from the table.' Her face was red. 'You'll want to get on with looking out your things. For tomorrow.'

As I returned to my room, their voices dropped ominously low. Well, *somebody* had to tell them, to open their eyes to what was so patently obvious to an outsider, which I would always be: the folly and hypocrisy which they, sad souls, were living among.

Aunt Nessie tapped on my door to say good-night. By the time I opened the door she had switched off the lamp in the hall and was going into her own room. This was the first night she hadn't made me my milky drink.

I sat on the edge of my bed for a long while. I had a headache from the sherry, and a thirst from the salty ham. I realised I was crumpling the pink candlewick; funny to think how only weeks ago I would have fretted about it, but now …

The taxi driver sounded his horn.

'Mr Dunnachie's put the case in, Neil. Is that us now?'

I took a last look round my bedroom.

'I'll tell him you're coming. Can you lock the front door behind you?'

I took two, three steps into the middle of the room. I bent my knees and pressed my weight down so that I could hear the errant floorboard creaking.

The music was the summer's memorial. But in the dressing-table mirror I looked like someone dancing on a grave.

At the station Aunt Nessie bought me a copy of *The Eagle* and a quarter-pound poke of boiled sweets – green 'soor plooms', with a hard outer coating of crystallised sugar and a soft centre that tasted of bitter lemon.

She leaned forward, so that I could kiss her. My kiss was rapid and business-like. I smelt swirly tea-roses from her, fragrant and enveloping. But she was holding herself more stiffly than on the day I'd arrived: as if she had learned in the interim how to be more protective of herself.

I stood at an open window of the carriage, waving down to her.

The train moved off.

Aunt Nessie grew smaller and smaller on the station platform.

I continued to stand at the window as we passed through Auchendrennan.

I had found the town grey, and I left it grey. In that sense nothing had changed. But I wasn't the same Neil Pritchard I'd been when the train had brought me south.

We followed the perimeter of Dalquhirk Bay. And then there was a very curious transformation. The sun appeared between lowering clouds, and the town – which was on the point of disappearing from view – turned from grey to silver. Auchendrennan shone – it dazzled – even against the vivid greens and blues, against the dark stormy sky arched over England and the fact of that constant concluding horizon.

Part Four

25

'Your room is ready for you,' my father announced rather ponderously on my arrival. My mother put her arm round my neck and embraced me, but she didn't kiss me.

It occurred to me that my father had shrunk by an inch or two; he couldn't have done, but I was confused nevertheless. My mother was all cheerfulness by comparison with him: maybe she was, or maybe she was pretending, which was another source of confusion to me.

'You've grown,' my mother said, and I blushed, taking care not to look at my father. She lifted my arm, and it was true, the sleeve of my jacket did appear to be shorter than before I'd left home. She let my arm drop, and it felt a yard long.

'So,' my father asked me, 'how was Kildrennan?'

At the best of times his Englishman's ignorance of our geography had exasperated my mother.

'Auchen-drennan,' she snapped.

'All right, Kay.'

She glared at him.

'You were missing Glasgow, I expect,' my mother said. 'Still, Nessie's a good sort.'

My father straightened his back, as if he was on parade in his uniform.

'Behaved yourself, Neil?' he asked me. 'Made some new friends?'

I didn't reply. I felt my face creasing with an expression of pain.

'Help him off with his coat, Eric.'

As he held up the collar and shoulders, I noticed little gummed labels stuck on some items of furniture. Some blue, some yellow.

'What are those stickers for?'

My mother repeated me.

' "What are – ?" ' She followed my eyes. 'Oh. Nothing.' She picked up her apron. 'I've put the kettle on. And I've baked you some pancakes.'

My father took my coat, placed it on the end of the banister. Neither of them had mentioned my rough new voice.

'Has your auntie been feeding you properly?' my father asked.

I nodded.

My mother bustled past us both.

'We don't want another talking-to on our Scottish diet, thank you very much.'

Clearly she did not intend the remark humorously.

'We need an extra chair, Eric. At the table.'

My father went off to fetch the chair.

I looked round. After less than five minutes in the house, following nearly eight weeks away, everything was already depressingly familiar. I recognised it all – the furniture, the pictures, the atmosphere – only too well.

The telephone started ringing in the living-room. My mother came out of the kitchen and went through to answer it. From the hall I couldn't fail to overhear her summons.

'Eric! Here …'

She handed over the receiver, not bothering to cover the mouthpiece.

'It's your office. Miss Wonderful again. Don't be long, for heaven's sake – '

The kettle was boiling in the kitchen, whistling through its spout.

' – I want us to have a nice tea, remember.'

I closed my eyes, tight shut, as if that way I might be able to obliterate it all, wipe it out.

Over the next days the questions I was asked about myself, about Auchendrennan, were cursory, and my answers not listened to. My mother didn't tell me that she'd had private conversations on the phone with Aunt Nessie. My father picked at his food and toyed with the teaspoon in his saucer and practised that old habit of reaching a hand up to his thinning hair, as if to check that he hadn't lost any more in the couple of minutes since last time. Everything was more or less the same, in other words, only it wasn't; this normality was being feigned, it was imitation, a pastiche.

At school I kept losing my train of thought.

The mention of Robert Louis Stevenson in an English class. The word 'cubile', 'lair', in a passage of Latin translation. An illustration of a peel tower in our Scottish History textbook. Chief exports of Italy.

My homework was regularly a dog's dinner. My marks plummeted.

156

Dad was away at the air base, so my mother went to the parents' night by herself. She returned home with a face like fizz.

'There are plenty of other boys who'd give their eye-teeth to have the chances you've had, Neil Pritchard. What's the matter with you? You'd better buck up, my lad.'

My father tried to smooth over the situation on his next visit home. I heard them talking about me in the kitchen.

'Keep your voice down, Kay, will you?'

'I don't need to be told what I should or shouldn't do in my own home.'

My father said he thought it might be something ' – well, you know – '

'No, I don't.'

'Well, *physical*. Because he's growing up. His voice.'

'Everyone has to grow up.'

'It's more difficult for some than – '

'It's difficult for me too. Knowing what to do about him. *You*'re not here.'

'It won't be for much longer. When are we going to tell him?'

'Don't you dare mention it. Not till we're quite ready.' She was pleading with him. 'D'you hear me, Eric?'

One evening it was Bone's voice I heard speaking through the rattly grille of our old wireless set.

Somehow he had found me, in our cramped living-room.

I was appalled.

It was the repeat of a broadcast transmitted in the spring.

'... I can't imagine working anywhere else but here. Auchendrennan, and round and about. I don't know what it is, this Solway landscape gets into your soul. How this scenery shifts. Water, land. Quicksands. The Deil's Lair.'

His enthusiasm was prodigious.

I stared at the wireless.

I listened to him, transfixed.

'The sinking sands. The bits that are sometimes water, sometimes land. The greenness of the fields – brilliant really green green – and the salt water meadows. The reeds rattling, the cries of the marsh birds ...'

The words gave way to his music. It was the very spirit of Dalquhirk, Rosmailzie.

My mother asked me vaguely, 'Who was that composer Nessie was talking about? The one you got to meet?'

'Just – just someone,' I croaked out.

'What did you have to do? Sing for him?'

'Sometimes.'

'I hope he appreciated you.'

My father turned the page of his newspaper. 'Rather a precarious occupation. Music. Not a proper career, I mean.'

My mother shot him A Look.

'Isn't there any other music we could be listening to, Eric? Something with a tune to it?'

★

I received a small package from Aunt Nessie.

It contained my Parker fountain pen, given to me when I'd passed the entrance exam to my school; a Mary Renault paperback; several coins; a handkerchief, which had been washed and ironed.

Skerryvore
17 Hauselock Avenue
AUCHENDRENNAN
Tel. Auchendrennan 1524

28th September '62

My Dear Neil,

I found these bits and pieces when I was cleaning your room, and so I'm returning them to you.

I hope you've settled back into your Glasgow ways by now. How is it at school? The house feels very quiet without you, you know!!

There is little to report, I'm afraid. We've still had no sighting of Mr Bone. I gather that Mr Maitland is looking rather haggard these days. My source also tells me that the doctor prescribes several tablets, to help him sleep and so forth. How different it all was earlier, in the summer, when you first came to us.

I trust that you were able to take away some happy memories from Auchendrennan.

Do please remember me to both your parents, won't you?

My kind regards to them, and to yourself.

A.N. (Smeaton)

★

I collected as many photographs of Bone and Maitland as I could.

I went into the Mitchell Library in town and surreptitiously tore several out of, first, books in the Music Room, and then – chasing up references in a bibliography – from newspapers I had called up from the stacks in a false name. I kept them at home safe between the pages of this or that reference book in my room which I thought my mother was unlikely to look into.

If I'd had the funds I would have bought a couple of LPs of Bone's music, but I didn't manage more than going into the record shop every time I passed and fetching out the empty covers from the racks. My courage didn't reach to smuggling out those awkwardly-sized cardboard sleeves with their studio-portrait shots of Bone.

One small square photograph I found in the *Radio Times*, and another in *The Scotsman*; I cut them out and carefully put them away.

When I realised the two men had featured in a poster for the previous year's Edinburgh Festival, I wrote to the publicity office, offering to pay whatever was required to obtain a poster for myself, but I didn't receive a reply from them. (I was especially aggrieved, because I had included a small stamped self-addressed envelope to encourage a speedy response.)

I taught myself to smoke as Bone had – occasionally – smoked.

I placed the cigarette in the corner of my mouth, then flicked the switch of the lighter (shoplifted from a dingy tobacconist's; so far had I fallen from grace). I inclined my head, to catch the flame. When the flame had died I closed the palm of my hand round the lighter, simultaneously screwing up my eyes in readiness for the first cloudlets of smoke. Only then did I swivel the cigarette forward between my lips.

I lit up in back lanes near the school – and for bravado's sake on Great Western Road, after compulsory rugby practice, while I waited for a blue double-decker out to our suburb. I didn't dare to risk smoking at home, because my mother's nose was too keenly tuned to deceive her with any stronger disguising smell – Cow Gum with the lid left off or wintergreen or the linseed oil my father used on his cricket bat.

But she must have suspected. Perhaps she caught the traces in the weave of my school pullover, just as back in my bedroom at the bungalow I had smelt cheroots and cigars from Slezer's Wark. I may simply have *looked* guilty, and guileful.

★

A postcard from Aunt Nessie.

... and I saw Mr Maitland myself. He was looking quite a bit older. Jacket buttons in wrong buttonholes. Not even a hanky in his top pocket! Shoes very dusty, and a trailing shoelace.

Later I got to hear what Auchendrennan already knew.

Mrs Faichnie had returned one day to Slezer's Wark, but not at Maitland's summons. He was still living there alone.

She started tidying up, which acted as a provocation to him. She found he'd been in her larder, nothing was where it usually was, and she told him off. Plates of half-eaten food had been left up and down the house, and she grumbled about the mess.

'If you hate it so much, Mrs Faichnie, go somewhere else. I don't need *you* moaning at me. *You* don't know your place, that's the problem.'

He'd always been talked about as a gent, one of the old school. But gents, of any school, didn't talk about people knowing their place. That riled her. Maybe he'd just forgotten himself, or maybe she was seeing the true Maitland. She wasn't bothered about discovering which.

She took off her apron and tossed it on to the kitchen table.

Maisie Faichnie had reached her Rubicon.

26

A Sunday afternoon in our suburb.

It was one of my father's 'home' weekends.

We'd had lunch, eaten with Family Favourites on in the background to patch over the long silences between us. Later on in the afternoon, Semprini Serenade. Then, Sing Something Simple.

Sundays were deadly. Reams of homework, hours of the stuff, and always a home-reader to be getting on with if by any chance you had time left on your hands.

I felt heavy after the broth and the steak pie and potatoes and then the rice pudding.

Mid-afternoon now I had another ritual. I pushed a chair against my bedroom door, unhooked the mirror from the wall, crouched beneath the window sill and watching myself in the mirror glass, took down my trousers.

From upstairs I heard the kitchen door being slammed. Then the front door was shut.

It sounded like the wind's doing, but there was no wind today.

I moved across to my bedroom window. My mother was out on the pavement, pushing her arms into the sleeves of her tweed coat. She was making off at speed, past the Dochertys', in the direction of Dunglass Road. She was in her sturdy shopping shoes, although there were no shops open on a Scottish Sunday; those heels clopped, not like her best court shoes for visiting which pecked at the cement, or her in-between off-to-town heels which (because they were half-a-size too big) rattled.

She was meaning to go for a long walk, I guessed. By herself.

I sat down on the edge of the bed, where the mattress sagged.

The flowery spirals of blue on the beige carpet led me into a bower of roses and thorns, beauty and hurt, the sanctified life of Slezer's Wark and my abrupt expulsion from it.

I found my father in our dinette. He was zealously polishing two pairs of shoes, one black and one brown.

It took him a few moments to realise I was standing there. He looked up, then lowered his eyes again.

He seemed ill-at-ease with me in the room, just the two of us.

'Where's Mum?' I asked.

'She's gone out.'

'To see Gran?'

'I don't know where she's gone.'

He continued rubbing in brown polish with the brown polish brush.

'When will she be back?'

He didn't reply.

'You'll have to be careful with the polish, Dad. So you don't get any on the carpet.'

'Just what your mother told me.' He nodded at his feet. 'I've put newspaper down.'

I sidled past him, stopped in front of the dining-table. Several loose sheets of newspaper were lying on top. On one of them my eye was caught by a number of crosses inked against small ads under the heading 'SINGLES' FLATS TO LET'.

I went back down to the living-room later.

My father was sitting by the unlit gas fire. He had the newspaper open on his lap, but he wasn't reading it. He didn't come out of his thoughts straightaway.

'Neil –'

'Hi, Dad.'

'Not doing your homework – ?'

'When will Mum be back?'

He looked at his watch.

'She'll be … For our tea, I imagine. Yes, back for tea.'

He folded up the newspaper.

I didn't move.

'Is there something – ?'

'I thought I saw Mr Duggan the other day,' I said, launching in. 'In town.'

I hadn't seen him. But I had to get my father's acquaintance introduced into the conversation somehow.

'Oh yes?'

'What does he do in the police?'

'He's an Inspector.'

'Where did you meet him?'

'At – at the Lodge.'

'I think it was him,' I said.

'In his uniform?'

' I …' I hadn't anticipated this detail, rehearsing the scene upstairs in my bedroom. '… I can't remember.'

Pause.

'Dad – ?'

'Yes?'

I swallowed. It was an accidental effect, also unplanned.

Back to the script in my head.

'What if you felt …'

'Yes?'

'… something had happened – that shouldn't have happened – '

'What kind of thing, son?'

'A man – an older man …'

I let a silence follow.

'What's this about, Neil?'

'I'm not supposed to tell.'

'But – you think you should? Tell me?' My father sounded apprehensive. 'Or – or tell someone else?'

'The police?'

'Well, I don't know. It – it depends what it is.'

'In Auchendrennan – ' I began.

'Something happened there?'

'You know about the singing?'

'At that composer's?'

'Euan Bone,' I said.

'It's got to do with him?'

My father pulled himself up in the chair. He was staring at me.

'What happened, Neil?'

I was trying to remember the lines I'd been preparing for the past hour.

'There's a word,' I said. ' "Homosexual".'

I heard my father catch his breath.

'Yes.' He spoke drily. 'Yes, there is.'

'It's against the law, though, isn't it?'

'This – ' My father cleared his throat. ' – this involves you in some way?'

163

'He picked me.'

'Picked you? To sing?'

Pause.

The colour rose on my father's face.

'Not – not just to sing?'

'We went up to Rosmailzie Forest,' I said, speeding myself up. 'And we went swimming. In Dalquhirk Bay.' The rehearsed words had come back to me, they were tumbling out. 'We lay in the dunes, or on the rocks. Then he took me swimming. So we had to take showers afterwards. He said. We went back to the house. And took our clothes off. And ...'

Pause.

'What – what then?'

I didn't speak.

'Neil?'

My father's voice had recovered its strength.

'Mr Duggan,' I said, 'Inspector Duggan – he would have to know about it, wouldn't he?'

'Know what, Neil?'

'About what happened. What he did.'

'What did Bone do?'

I gulped down breath before continuing.

'When his friend was away,' I said. 'Mr Maitland.'

My father was waiting. The room fell utterly silent.

Keep to the script.

'In the shower. In the wood. In the music room.'

Pause.

'In his bedroom,' I said.

Before he left the next day, after lunch and a couple of phone calls, my father merely told me – as he was bending down to pick up his travel bags – that the business we'd been discussing was 'in hand'. He spoke out of my mother's hearing. He didn't wait for a reply from me.

I didn't really give it any more thought.

Not that I forgot what I'd done. But as soon as I'd said what I said on Sunday afternoon, I deliberately – insistently – despatched the matter to a back room of my mind.

The ramifications didn't occur to me. By mentioning Mr Duggan, I had only meant to give my father a reason for listening to me; the Inspector was my alibi, the cover and guarantee for my fiction.

How could my father leave us now? My fantasy included him too. It was a web I'd spun to protect ourselves, to keep the Pritchards safe. All I'd intended by it was to try to reel my father in, and to stop our three lives from unravelling.

I *was* aware that I wasn't thinking of something. That not-thinking seemed to be a necessary quarantine. What I failed to realise, though, was that by the same determined effort of will I was sidestepping all the tedious, footling inconveniences of guilt.

My father suddenly moved out.

'It'll make things easier for your mother.'

I didn't see how.

'Don't go, Dad.'

He had wrong-footed *me*, I was the one outmanoeuvred.

'For a few months. You can come and visit. Then – then I'll probably go back down south to work.'

The furniture with blue stickers attached – his share of the spoils – went with him, initially into storage.

'And good riddance,' my mother said, either about the furniture or her husband, or both.

Immediately afterwards an estate agent called in to see us. A number of viewers rang the door bell, and my mother breezily showed them round. An offer was made for the house, not a very good one, but it was accepted.

'A quick sale. We'll be out by Christmas,' my mother said with satisfaction.

I was stunned.

'See who's had all the hard work to do?' my mother asked me. 'It's a man's world all right.'

I moved with my mother to a small flat in a block of six in Kelvindale.

It was a decent neighbourhood – 'all owner-occupiers', my mother reminded her visitors – but it lacked poetry.

We had venetian blinds put up at the windows. When I prised the slats apart, I looked out at a prospect of canal, the Clyde and Forth. The tow-path, a lock. Untidy scrub. The gas works a quarter-of-a-mile away.

165

My mother acquired a fresh hairstyle.

She had grown her hair over the summer. Now she got it piled up and combed out. A kind of bouffant. I wasn't sure that the style suited her. I felt that she had her doubts too, judging from the number of times in a day when she would glance into a mirror or search for herself in the glass of a picture frame.

She took to varnishing her nails. Soft pink, Coral Atoll. I hated the harsh smell of the varnish from the open bottle, it seemed to set up a little panic in my throat, an airlock.

My father was sharing a house with a couple of Air Force colleagues, on the Edinburgh side of the city.

One Saturday I was allowed to take a train out.

The atmosphere in the house was much more relaxed than I was expecting. There were bottles of French wine in the kitchen, and a Percy Faith LP lying on top of the record player.

I didn't tell my mother about the wine, or about the laughter from the others, or about live-wire Jeanette, who'd driven over to collect Malcolm and Kenny and who cheerily called my father 'E-ric-o'.

My mother plied me with questions about my visit, and I convinced myself I was being discreet not evasive in my answers. 'Uh-*hu* – ?' she kept saying, with an identical little question mark in her voice every time, and the hope that I might tell her more. I caught her watching me in the tinted mirror which hung above the electric fire, as if she was expecting my reflection there would tell her a different story.

27

[From *The Euan Bone Compendium*, ed. Farraday, publ. Bodley Head, London, 1984; Norton, New York 1986.]

There are only diary entries for the last weeks, when Bone was away from Auchendrennan, during that largely involuntary exile.

He speaks in his own voice, conducting a dialogue with himself. There's little information to be gleaned about his work; he's trying to discover how he can work, with his life now so unsettled.

*

I've written again to D.

The ms. was found, I said, <u>The L-Bs</u> is safe, & that's what matters. And we should agree not to talk about it. We've all done things in haste, I said, & regretted them later.

Wh. is why I don't want the situation to go on any longer like this. Will he give me a call – please?

I told him I'm still at Grizel's.

I don't know why I gave him my house keys that afternoon. I was telling him, it's up to <u>you</u>, if I come back or not.

Did he take the wrong inference – that it meant I wasn't intending to come back?

The house is in <u>his</u> name. It's mine to inherit, when he dies, but it was bought with M. money, and technically at the moment it <u>is</u> his.

The potential for misunderstanding is endless.

It was Elspeth's idea (in cahoots with Grizel?) to get me away from Auchendrennan for a while. I'm not so sure. I feel I've worsened something that cd. have been repaired more easily.

But he still won't answer the phone, and he hasn't replied to the 2nd letter, and I don't want to ask Grizel or Hamish to speak to him for me.

He still has the keys.

Ran gave me the garden flat in Glasgow for however long I needed it. But the view of dank rhododendrons overwhelmed me with sadness. A rowan tree by a house is supposed to ward off witches, but that one was too gloomy to bear.

Edinburgh is better. The Crescent is somehow v. Elizabeth Bowen, can't have changed much since WW 2. Can just glimpse the Forth and green Fife from the attic rooms. But I've forgotten how to work in a city, & Moray's phone never stops ringing.

Ming & Andro came round for a Serious Discussion. They think – and Dennis agrees – I need to get back on to a platform. (Waverley or Haymarket? said I, only half-joking.) They think it'll take my mind off things, better than sitting at a desk with brain fucked up.

I don't know.

Meanwhile … I've enquired about a cottage in St Andrews. The sea again, & dunes, & the links; the splendour falls on castle walls, & never better than at sunset.

Bone continued to work on his friends, to plead his case with Maitland for him if they could.

Maitland meantime was in the Home Counties, circling London, and proving very hard to pin down. He would keep one postal address ahead of Bone's mediators. Telephone calls weren't returned; letters arrived too late and went unanswered.

The Lantern Bearers. It won't go away, it nags at me. Frets and worries me that there's so much done, but ¼ still left. I'm going to lose it, I know I am.

I see the boys, with their blowing cloaks & their lanterns, out there in the darkness – first in Edinburgh, now in St Andrews where they've pursued me – they're waiting for me to be done with them, so they can grow up & live as men & die. They wave at me with their 2d lanterns, standing waiting, waiting.

I can't hear it, tho', the resolution – I need the voice. Without the voice I can't complete the last ¼, & without that The L-Bs doesn't exist, & the boys go on waiting & their wax candles burn perpetually in the dark.

Grizel is adamant, she says D.'s in London.

Colin tells me it's only en route to somewhere else. They spoke on the phone; at that point D. was staying at Basil Street, among the hotel's dowagers.

That was 3 days ago,

Last night I dreamed of Portofino. Is D. headed there?

Why should I have dreamed it if he isn't??

The boys follow me. By the cold dark North Sea. On the long ness shore. Among the waving dune grass. The glow of their lanterns in the dark. The waves crashing in, spume flying, the wind roaring like an invisible lion.

I'll need to find a voice: a voice in imitation of Neil's.
His voice was the same as the other voice that preceded it, in London, Simon's. I only realise that now. There is only one voice. The original & archetype. I've heard it twice. But shall I ever hear it again?

The L-Bs.
'Lost Innocence'.
Needing to grow up. Disillusionment. (Corruption, of course.)
But the door has closed.
Only, in imagination ... (The key to unlock the door.)

I'm still there. At S.'s Wark, in the music room. It's that piano I'm playing, the Bösendorfer, not any other. I'm listening to him/it singing. The voice. The one & only voice.

Liam says there was a sighting of D. in Bournemouth. At the Green Park, wh. is why I believe it. A bout of queasy Jewish taste in decor, all that gilt & ormolu, & it'll send him back north chastened. Maybe.
But that was a week ago.

Time doesn't stop.
Soon everything will fall back into place. It'll have been an interlude, one we don't refer to.
(Probably there are explanations, but I shan't seek them.
There's too little time for that.
Always it's this – a question of time.)

Should I finish the old clarinet piece for Fischer, or try to knock the Jamie the Saxth tunes into shape? (Piano? Harp? Plus another?)
If I'm working ...
Keep busy.

Bone wrote to Maitland (who was still incommunicado) at Auchendrennan, suggesting they might give some recitals together. A pushy theatrical agent had already been discussing dates and venues available at short notice, but Bone preferred to be a little more circumspect, even with time so limited.

Maitland didn't respond. In fact, he was on his way to Italy, to Portofino where he spent Christmas and saw in the New Year.

The agent had entered into negotiations with an American promoter, and several dates were organised for January: performances in Boston, Philadelphia, Washington, New York, and the campus at Cambridge, Massachusetts.

(There was talk of an American breakthrough at last. Bone, like Maitland, had long hoped for it.)

Additional concerts, postponed to permit the American itinerary, were rescheduled for February: in Belfast, Cardiff, Edinburgh, Glasgow and Aberdeen.

Agreements were required immediately. Maitland still couldn't be contacted. In the event, the cellist's role had to be offered elsewhere; Bone went along with the suggestion that it should be offered first to someone who had benefited from Maitland's tuition in the past – and who more talented, as (almost) all concurred, than a young Australian player called Paul Quigley.

Quigley accepted at once, expressing his gratitude for the opportunity. The itinerary was confirmed. Bone wrote to Maitland, explaining the situation. (He'd thought over everything, but a decision had needed to be made very quickly. The public, he added, knew that these were Douglas Maitland pieces, so he would be there with them in spirit, even though on the dozen or so occasions ahead someone else would be playing them.)

The cufflinks are the ones D. gave me. We chose these shoes together. I can't get hold of Russian Caravan, wh. has always been his favourite tea.

Dozens of times a day something reminds me.

I miss having him here. But in another sense he's everywhere.

America. It's what he always wanted for me.

Having Paul about like this so much, I know what will happen. I know I won't be able to help myself. He'll tell me, D. will never get to know, what harm can it do, & anyway why hasn't he tried to get in touch with you?

Sex will be a distraction from everything else I'm thinking. It'll solve nothing. But the nights will pass more quickly for it.

Portofino was a mistake.

Maitland might have gone there imagining he could console himself, but he ended up even more alone than in Auchendrennan.

Without Bone there, he was reminded of all that it used to mean to them.

Their friends were spending Christmas and New Year elsewhere. The nights in his hotel room were so long, but not in the sexy way when they were sharing the bed. Dawn came up slowly over the mountains, delaying and delaying.

Along the waterfront the awnings were raised. The Luna had closed its terrace for the season. The houses stared desolately at their reflections in the harbour water. A boat had spilled oil, not much but enough to spread a greasy purplish sheen on the surface.

Rain clouds blew up from Corsica. Maitland was feeling worse aches in his joints than he ever did in the middle of a Solway winter. By the fifth day he had to summon an osteopath to get him out of bed, his back was a rack of such searing pain.

28

My mother had gone back to work.

She'd found a secretarial job in an advertising agency in town. The others who worked there were quite a lively lot. They discussed what had been on television the night before; sometimes it was ITV, which my mother preferred we didn't watch (advertising breaks or not) because it was déclassé.

She told her friends, and had largely convinced herself, that she'd won back her independence. But, seeing the tiredness that drained her face and counting the Alka-Seltzers she was getting through in a week, I guessed differently.

My mother wanted us to be modern, and hire purchase assisted her.

Teak. Orange lampshades on driftwood bases. A squiggly shape of plain and tinted-blue mirror on the wall. A rattan screen, which stood in one corner of the open-plan living-room unused. Bead curtains through to the kitchen. A Creda washing machine, and a Morphy-Richards pop-up toaster. A small Frigidaire. A television set from DER, with a 17-inch screen.

My mother was visiting neighbours one Sunday evening, and left me on my own.

I pulled open the sliding doors on the television. I turned the 'on' switch and waited for the set to warm up. A picture appeared. I changed channels to the commercial one, which my mother thought was so vulgar.

'Sunday Night at the London Palladium'.

After Beat The Clock it was time for the top of the bill.

Liberace.

He was wearing a sequined tuxedo and white trousers and white shoes. A dazzle of rings. He sat at a colossal white piano. One rippling arpeggio cascaded into another.

Chopin, allegedly.

It was compelling to look at, and that must have been the point: you didn't listen to Liberace, you watched him.

His smile. The crackleglaze of lines around his eyes. The jet-black waved hair. The loose wrists, the supple hips as he shimmied forward to the edge of the stage.

He was sending himself up. He was also laughing at the audience.

I was bemused. A-mused, and repelled. I wanted to protect him, but he could control two thousand people, and an entire prime-time television viewership, and he also confused me because I couldn't take my eyes off the figure in frills and rhinestone trim filling our 17-inch screen to larger than life.

★

It was announced in the *Glasgow Herald* that there would be a recital at the St Andrews Halls by Euan Bone and Paul Quigley on February 23rd.

I mentioned it to my mother. When she saw how keen I was to go, she suggested she buy me a ticket as a birthday present in advance.

The ticket was bought: one seat, Back Stalls, Row N.

I was allowed to go into town for the evening by myself, the first time it had ever happened.

[From the *Compendium* diaries]
The usual ritual. Complan – enthroned on the po – then a big meal. Nothing changes. I'm standing in the wings, frozen. Somehow I get on to the stage, cross to the piano, only because I'm somewhere else entirely and this is someone else, not me.

At some point, miraculously the panic subsides. The fingers pressing on the keys, squeezing out the notes, I recognise them, & the phrases of music, as familiar to hear as my heartbeat.

Nothing changes.

Except that it's not him *playing with me. There's no Douglas. I can't think my way around that.*

The Hall was very busy. Some of the audience were in evening dress. At my mother's insistence I was wearing my school uniform. The talk around me was social, not musical; pocket diaries were taken out, lunch and dinner dates pencilled in.

Glasgow, 23.ii.63
45 minutes to go.

It's always strangest here, in Glasgow. At the St Andrew's Halls. I remember coming here just after the War, when there were concerts again. I devoured it all, whatever there was to hear.

And then I wanted to paint all the world with my own music. I wanted to turn all my feelings into sound. It was what I lived for, that & nothing else.

This is where I'm expected to show what I've achieved. The person I was is sitting at the back of the hall, in the darkness, & I'm performing for him. D. ought to be here too, because the music is for him to play, but – notwithstanding – it will carry. The young man will be sitting in the darkness where I can't see, and he'll be judging. I shall play to that spot, awaiting his verdict on me & the music of my life so far.

From my seat I held my breath as Bone stepped out on to the stage; he was followed by his partner for the evening, Quigley. They were both wearing black tails and white waistcoats and white bow-ties. We applauded as they made their way towards a gleaming grand piano and a cello resting against a chair.

I wondered again why Maitland wasn't here, when he and Bone were famous for the intensity of their recital performances.

But could the music they made together have been any more intense than what I was to hear that evening?

I sat enthralled.

The programme was Bone, Brahms, Bone, Bach, Bartok, Bone, Biber (transposition) – and for the two encores, Bone again. All the Bs, probably by no accident.

I watched rapt.

As they played, their two spirits seemed to be fused in the intimacy of their technique. Their two heads, fair and blond, dropped simultaneously. Now and then they smiled directly at one another, as if they were surprising even themselves.

I felt transported. To Budapest and Vienna and Augsburg, of course, but also to Auchendrennan. I remembered Slezer's Wark, and this time with pride – the privilege of going there to sing, under the tutelage of someone who had never played the soul out of the piano quite like this.

I clapped at the end till my hands hurt.

174

In the foyer I heard the couple in front of me tell another that they were going round to the stage-door.

I decided instantly to do the same.

A small crowd of acolytes and well-wishers had gathered on the street, by a lamppost. The rain was off. They were expectant, excitable; I could imagine the hiss of static from those fur jackets and silk-collared dinner jackets.

The door opened, and a delighted cry went up. Two men came out. The first was an employee of the theatre, the second was Quigley. The cellist, with gathering confidence, started to speak from the top step, back-lit.

He thanked the throng for their presence. He singled out the inner core who had extended an invitation to dinner.

'My friends – Euan is very tired tonight. Too tired for supper.'

Voices were raised in disappointment.

'But – but I should very glad to accept. Although I realise it won't be the same for you.'

Expressions of relief, a small round of applause.

The Restaurant One-o-One, someone called out.

Another asked, 'You're quite sure Mr Bone won't manage – ?'

'*Quite* sure. He'll go back to the hotel.'

'Dinner is booked,' someone said.

Quigley smiled, opened his arms to them.

'Ladies and gentlemen, I'm delighted. Let the festivities commence!'

Another, louder round of applause.

I didn't want to go home just yet, so I walked on into town.

I reached the grid of straight streets that run down from Blythswood Hill, lined by soot-streaked commercial palazzi built either in the style of Turin or Chicago. In the darkness they were more than ever like sandstone canyons; I tried to make out the rooftop caryatids and other mythical creatures seven or eight storeys above me.

It had started to rain again. I buttoned my school coat and buckled the belt, and ran on, jumping over puddles.

I'd heard them talking about the Central Hotel. As I cut across Bothwell Street my eye was caught by some kind of activity taking place in a back lane. A car was parked, with its lights off; figures were moving in front of it.

I made out police uniforms. It was a police car.

One of the back doors opened. Another man got out, while his arm was held by one of the policemen; he was wearing civvies.

A youth, really.

He started to walk off. Someone whistled him back. The car's boot lid was raised, an object was removed – an umbrella – and handed to him.

I steeled myself to follow.

The youth stopped across the street from the hotel, sheltering beneath the umbrella. He was badly dressed, he looked thin and white-faced and hunched.

What was he waiting for?

He straightened himself when a taxi drew up under the entrance portico of the hotel. The uniformed doorman was occupied inside the building, and the taxi's passenger in light-coloured raincoat was fully visible to me as he got out.

It was Bone.

The youth ran across the street, dodging the cars with their windscreen blades slapping.

He approached Bone, said something to him as Bone turned away. Bone stopped. He looked about.

The youth held the umbrella over them both. He nodded down the street.

Bone hesitated briefly. He deliberated for a few moments.

Then he made his decision.

The two of them walked off past the hotel entrance, sharing the umbrella.

I watched, feeling rain trickle down the back of my neck. I could feel dampness coming up through the soles of my shoes.

On the Gordon Street flank of the hotel I saw another police car driving in beneath the station canopy. It flashed its headlights twice, then reverted to side-lights. On Hope Street opposite, a car – unmarked, anonymous – replied, switching its headlights on and off twice.

I could still see Bone, or his burberry. His head was obscured by the umbrella. The youth was too shadowy to distinguish properly.

From somewhere behind me I heard a single loud guffaw of knowing male laughter.

Hope Street crosses Argyle Street, under the old glassed railway bridge

176

called the Highlandman's Umbrella, and on a right turn becomes Jamaica Street. Jamaica Street, with its iron-built Venetian warehouses, leads to the river. Behind Jamaica Street are other streets of lesser warehouses and a warren of side-roads and lanes, the furthest within a couple of hundred yards of the Clyde.

I looked at my watch. It was getting very late. Half-past ten. I was wet from the rain. But I couldn't give up just yet.

I turned up my collar, just as Bone and the youth had done with theirs. I ran after them, along the darker side of Hope Street, towards Jamaica Street, beneath the massive baronial walls of the hotel.

And on towards the river, away from the respectable quarter.

At one point Bone stopped and turned round, he started walking back. The youth followed at his side, talking. Whatever he said must have persuaded Bone. They both turned round again, under cover of the umbrella, and they continued on their way. The youth led by no more than a couple of steps, so that he was able to keep talking to his companion.

I ran after them. I was keeping twenty or thirty yards behind, so that I wouldn't be seen if they looked back.

I trailed them down streets I didn't know.

The rain was easing off, to drizzle.

I had to watch for trolley buses on their wires. Once a car blared its horn at me, and I thought that was bound to make them look round, but I was lucky.

Bone was being urged on, lured forward, by all the youth's ready promises.

I was crossing the entrance to a lane when I caught a movement in the corner of my eye, as I'd done earlier. But when I looked into the narrow gulch between the old dingy buildings, the space was empty, except for dustbins and a disintegrating pile of wet cardboard boxes. A spouting drainpipe hung loose from a wall, beating time.

I set off again, quicker than before, so that I wouldn't lose them. The street we were on was quieter, but I saw the lights of a pub at the end. I started to hear voices. Laughter, singing, some shouts.

I didn't see what any of this had to do with Euan Bone. To me Slezer's Wark had been a perfect paragon of refinement and civilised life, and whenever I thought of it I saw in my mind's eye sunshine and abundant light. Even at my most despondent I remembered the brightness of the rooms, the gracious ambience, our distance there from the ordinary.

177

Things had led us both to *this*. A dark street of unlit warehouses, a flickering streetlight. The smell of the river. A cracked pavement, and shards of broken bottle, a sodden newspaper clogging a drain. The few cars, parked where the one functioning lamppost could illuminate them, were as matter-of-fact and mundane as Maitland's cars had been rare and exotic. A mongrel with a curly tail pissed against the back wheel of one.

I'm hurrying down the deserted street after them. I shall always be hurrying down that street after them. Bone and the youth. The pub's lights shine out on to the greasy pavement at the corner. A tin signboard, shaped like a pewter pot, projects from the wall. On one of the high windows a lacy cavalier in a feathered hat – a cardboard cut-out of a head and upper torso – is raising a tankard, another pewter pot. There are voices. Laughter, singing, some shouts. An argument. Fucking this, fucking that. Fucking fuck yersel', y'cunt.

There are always those voices, laughing and singing and angrily bawling out.

Above them, although I wasn't aware of hearing it at the time, there's the squawk of a seagull, circling overhead on a late-night scavenging mission. However many times I relive these moments, I always hear the gull, its screech sounding like a frantic warning.

They must have gone inside the pub.

My fear was that Bone would look back, over the pane of frosted glass in the high-silled window, and see me. Maybe I was afraid for Maitland's sake, at a betrayal: afraid of discovering more about Bone than I wanted to know.

I waited outside, by the swing doors, trying to see in. Then I crossed the street, hoping to get a view inside from there. I saw nothing, but I was well out of the way of the rough arms and elbows pushing in and the drunks staggering out.

Bone had been cheated into coming here. Why else *would* he have come?

And for what purpose exactly?

I had never really *known*. About male sex. Six months on I was no better informed than I'd been then. I had spoken to my father in our living-room from the unprofound depths of my ignorance. I'd been guided merely by a feeling, I'd gone on a hunch that started between my legs, in my scrotum.

They didn't reappear, Bone and the youth. I waited for half-an-hour in the lightening drizzle, forty minutes.

178

The nearest streetlight was on the blink all that time.

I was sure I couldn't have missed them, and so I supposed they were still inside. It didn't occur to me that Bone might have left the premises by another door.

Customers came and went. At one point a car drew up, a smarter car, and the passenger went in through the swing doors and fetched out another two men from inside, as shabbily dressed as their fellow drinkers but quite familiar with getting nimbly into a Ford Zephyr. Apart from that, there was nothing else to notice.

I pictured the flat in Kelvindale. My mother, with work to go to tomorrow, would be sitting up expecting me to walk in any minute now with an excuse for her before I got down to describing my evening. Tonight I was out by myself on appro. If I wanted to go off into town again after curfew, I couldn't spend any longer here.

Very reluctantly I started out on my journey home.

My head was full of the evening, and I wasn't concentrating on how I got back.

The walk along the Broomielaw next to the river, up Jamaica Street to Union Street. A late bus out to the West End and along Great Western Road.

The patrician Victorian terraces passed in a blur. I was replaying the past several hours: the concert, the scene at the stage-door, trailing Bone to the Central Hotel, the car headlights turning on and off in the lane, the badges glinting on police uniforms. Then, following Bone and the youth to the pub, and my ineffectual vigil there.

And all the while I was staring at my reflection in the bus window, while the dark night city glided behind it.

My mother looked up from her sewing.

'Oh, *there* you are.'

She had to remind herself that I ought to have been back an hour-and-a-half or more ago.

The telephone flex was fankled, so I knew she had been speaking to someone.

Quite a different matter was preying on her mind.

My father, I guessed: and *his* freedom. Or just possibly an office colleague, moving in on hers.

I got ready for bed. My mother was still sitting up when I passed her on my way to and from the bathroom, at half-past midnight.

She had asked me only one or two questions about the concert, and didn't hear me out when I tried to tell her. I was a little hurt by her lack of interest, but more than that I was relieved.

In bed, with the light out, it all came back to me. I was walking down the gloomy street again ...

And I am still.

I'm walking towards the pub lights shining out on to the greasy corner of pavement; towards the voices, the laughter and the singing and the oathing, the barrage of abuse. I'm still standing waiting across the street, by the flickering lamppost. A gull cries out from the darkness overhead, screaming down a warning ...

I always wake up. But only because I failed to wake up on that first night, 23 February 1963, and soon went to sleep and slept soundly, tired and quite complacent, as if I'd forgotten the terrible depravity of what I'd told my father, my unforgivable act of treachery.

I slept soundly in Kelvindale. And so, for the sake of my guilt, I *have* woken up ever since, every time I walk that same dim street in my night dreams.

29

I'd put my homework on to the sideboard and was setting the table for tea.

Twenty-four hours ago I'd been getting ready to set out for the recital. The television was on.

I laid out our cutlery. I still forgot it was for two, not three.

Pots were steaming away in the kitchen.

'Did you turn the mince down, son?'

'Yes, Mum.'

'Mince was something else your father took a right scunner to.'

My mother continued to varnish her nails. I finished setting the table. I looked out between the slats of the venetian blinds, at the canalside. It was quite scrubby. The gas works framed a fine sunset over the leafy roads of semi-detached Jordanhill two miles away.

I heard the voice from the television first. A mention of the name, 'Euan Bone'. I spun round.

The screen showed a small crowd of people. The facade of the Central Hotel. Paul Quigley.

'The musical community in Scotland and beyond has been paying tribute today to composer and pianist Euan Bone.'

'Mr Bone's body was discovered in his Glasgow hotel room by fellow-musician Paul Quigley in the early hours of this morning.'

'A hospital spokesman gave cause of death as "respiratory failure".'

'Shocked admirers gathered outside the hotel to express their condolences.'

'Close friend Douglas Maitland was too upset to speak to reporters from his Galloway home.'

'Euan Bone, at only thirty-seven years of age, had built a reputation in his native country second to none ...'

I was frozen still.

The pictures on the screen kept moving. Quigley, still wearing tails and with what might have been a blood stain on his white waistcoat, was shaking hands with a departing police officer. A woman in a fox pelt stole was crying into the back of her hand.

Somehow I took those two details in.

But I was too stunned to be aware of anything else. The blood was running cold in my veins. I felt I had a blade of ice stuck deep in my gut.

★

A week went past.

I can't account now for that week.

I was lost. I was out of it.

I went to school. I came home. I ate. I sat down to my homework. I went to bed and I slept.

I was only existing on the surface of things. I saw no more than what was immediately in front of me. I wasn't looking down or behind.

A week is missing from my history, because for a week I refused to think.

30

The funeral was delayed. It went out on the Scottish news on television, condensed to two or two and a half minutes.

A service in old St Kentigern's, where they played some of Bone's music. The mourners made their way outside, led by an elderly ashen man with a stoop – Maitland, I realised with a shock. At his side was a woman I didn't recognise, who might have been Bone's sister. I saw Grizel Langmuir, accompanied by a girl-friend, and there was just a glimpse of Mrs Faichnie, who was slipping a handkerchief behind her glasses. Then a shot of the kirk minister, and his toothy, poppy-eyed wife from the Happy Families' card.

Shots of the cemetery. Figures by an open grave, coffin being lowered. (The commentary informed us that the grave had been lined with reeds from the marshes – cue, a close-up.) On the coffin, a spray of white arum lilies, the one flower I associated with those fragrant airy rooms at Slezer's Wark.

I was still staring at the screen when a photograph was shown later in the news.

I was jolted out of my trance.

A young man with a sharply, foxily handsome face. Powerful shoulders and a solid neck.

An accidental association, I thought at first. But I *did* recognise him.

It was the stranger on Auchendrennan beach I'd trailed, along Yett Street.

Name, McPherson. Arrested by police officers investigating the recent spate of explosions. His nationalist credentials, and a record of petty crime. One of an 'active service' sect: based in Edinburgh, but drawing wider support.

The police were disclosing little else, except to say that searches would continue in different parts of Scotland.

I immediately forgot about McPherson. The shore walker.

It was the pictures of the funeral which stayed in my head all evening, and for many months to come. St Kentigern's Kirk, the minister's wife, Grizel Langmuir, Mrs Faichnie dabbing at her eyes, the coffin, the spray of white arum lilies.

I didn't sleep that night. The next night I got some light broken sleep. I dreamed I was in the cemetery. I was standing by that open grave lined with reeds; something made me turn round, and there was Bone standing behind me. He held a cup of tea, with a wedge of fruit cake balanced on the saucer, but he was only half-there – he had begun to rot away, and his skeleton stuck through the sere skin. His purplish gooseflesh fluttered in ribbons, a terrible rank breeze was blowing up from the hole in the ground –

I woke as I was tumbling out of bed but a split-second before I hit the floor. I lay on the rug staring into the skirting board, I heard my heart's hollow banging inside my chest, the blood thundering away in my head.

There's that something I'm not thinking of.
I don't remember.
It can't have happened.
One Sunday afternoon.
And the night following the concert.
I'm waiting for the damburst …

I took the bus to school and home again. I would catch glimpses of Auchendrennan in a shop doorway, or in sunlight on a roof, the angle of a wall, a cat's cradle of telegraph wires. Bits of the music would come floating back to me, The Lantern Bearers. I smelt damp wool and wet shoe-leather and I was back in St John's and St James's Kirk.

Off the bus, I would start running, but I could never run fast enough to get away from the pictures in my head. There wasn't any difference between what I visualised and the world called real. I was running along streets, past doorways and walls that might have been in Glasgow or in Auchendrennan, I was running through my dreams.

Which left me tired out in the morning, exhausted.
The school day lasted from half-past eight until four, with sports and corps and activities afterwards. I had to spread myself thinner and thinner.

I didn't come straight home at four o'clock, but trailed the city centre streets for an hour or two. I lifted a few books in Wylie's bookshop, from the sliding shelves, under the noses of the genteel assistants, and in Jackson's, in its classy sepulchral murk. They weren't books that I wanted; I only did it as a dare to myself.

I lit up a cigarette in the nearest back lane. I wasn't much good at smoking and practice didn't help, I kept choking and inhaling. Doing it (almost) out of sight defeated the purpose of the exercise, but I was too conspicuous in my chocolate brown and gold school uniform; anyone who saw was bound to phone in to the school office, and the culprit was expected to be honest enough to own up before the whole morning assembly.

My Dear Neil,

I've been meaning to write to you, ever since Euan Bone's things were brought back to Yett Street.

No one's seen much of Mr M. He does drive thru' Auchendrennan in his car, but he's always going somewhere else – or is he just driving round in circles?

Aileen Ross, who was a nurse (I think I told you?) and gets to hear these things, says that he has been prescribed tranquillisers, but by different doctors, so I can't say if he's in a fit state to drive or not.

I suppose we should be sorry for him, but he has always kept himself apart, and (the Bible is quite correct) you <u>do</u> reap what you sow.

You may feel that this is now a long while ago. You will probably have started to forget, and have lots of new interests to keep you busy. People's stories are more interesting to folk of my age, because the young want excitement. Even <u>I</u> did, once upon a time, if you can believe that – and look what happened to me!

Maybe I shall hear from you again one of these days?

Mr Donnet from down the road – who lost his wife – is coming in at any moment with his seed tray for me.

Kind Regards,

Yours aye,

Aunt Nessie (Smeaton)

I would lie on my bed staring up at the ceiling. I knew every hillock and whorl in the chipboard paper, gloss-painted light tan.

I tried to float free. Levitation. Nothing to hold me.

I couldn't manage for more than a second or two. Or perhaps not at all. I was pulled back by strings, I was held by guy-ropes. I was fettered and manacled.

There was no place to go, except to where I'd been so many times before, into sunlit green rooms and night-time streets cold with shadows.

My school report cards at the end of the term were distinctly unfavourable, and there was less talk now of my previous potential.

My mother made an appointment to see the Rector. She tried to apologise to him, hinting that things at home hadn't been easy for me. Afterwards I received her most serious dressing-down yet. She left me in no doubt that a private school had been well beyond her own and my father's expectations for themselves. As a scholarship boy, I should be particularly conscious of my situation. It showed bad breeding, she said, to be so churlish about using the opportunities which life presents.

'They'll boot you out, Neil, do you realise that? Then what will become of you?'

But I knew.

'You'll turn into some common little savage, that's what.'

Like the red-haired boy, spitting at strangers and leap-frogging his friends' backs on Auchendrennan beach.

My mother was in tears. However, that was all the hard talking I needed. Now that I understood how far I might fall, I had to start right now, working to save the rest of my life.

Maitland hadn't been able to make his peace with Bone.

That must have been his great sadness. He had lost him, but at the one point – after thirteen years – when they'd had a serious disagreement.

There would never be any redress now.

Maitland could only dwell on that fact in the loneliness of the weeks and months afterwards, marooned in the fastness of Slezer's Wark with his salvage of memories.

I could conjure the music back now, every phrase of it. A soundtrack to my footsteps, to the Glasgow traffic passing, to the restless play of sunlight and shadows on those temperamental spring days, alternately bright and overcast from minute to minute.

I slipped between the notes, slithered in and out between the words, inhabiting the music completely. An escape, briefly, which only brought me round again, to where I didn't want to be. The present or the past, there was no difference. Cul-de-sac, dead end.

'Your uniform cost me good money, Neil, keep it tidy and it'll return the favour, you'll look smarter. You're starting to slouch – back straight, hold your head up, and look folk in the eye. Remember, son, pick up your feet, you've forgotten about them down there, don't drag them – *lift!*'

I answered the phone one evening. It was my father. He spoke for a while, asked if I had any news for him. He didn't mention the name 'Euan Bone', or make any reference to the recent tragedy, or to my summer away either.

It might have happened, everything, in some parallel world to this one.

A white-faced youth. In some long dark trailing garment like a cloak. Beneath it, or a reflection trapped in the glass – a glimmer of light, a candle.

He was only there for a moment, at my bedroom window. A white-faced youth. I thought I was looking at myself.

He turned away, made off. It had been for just a couple of seconds, but I'd registered the wide staring eyes, and the terrible censoriousness of that wee shrunken mouth.

I shot out of bed.

The lantern bearers!

They'd been waiting for me all along, and here they were. I wasn't going to get away so easily.

In the next seconds they came flying at me. I beat at them with my arms, then covered my ears and eyes to protect myself, I tried to shut them out. But they knew me too well, they knew me inside out.

I blundered out of my bedroom. Out of the flat. Down the communal staircase.

On to the street.

I smelt the sea, the fish.

I turned in the direction of the harbour. I realised I had to defy them, somehow. But I was scared out of my wits.

I found myself in shrubbery, breaking branches. The ground sloped away, and I slid downhill, grabbing at gorse bushes to steer myself and scratching my arms and legs on the thorns.

187

I ran blindly across the road in the dusk, towards the dunes. A voice sounded behind me, a man's.

'Just get away from here, will you – ?'

I raced on through the long grass, over the soft sand.

After that I felt the shore wetter under my feet. The voice was still calling after me.

Ahead I could see some lights. Lantern-shine. Candles swinging in their little glass cases.

Cloaks blowing open and shut. Towering stove-hats pulled low over pallid faces. The hugger-mugger of limbs.

I smelt fire. Charred wood. Apples baked in their crackly skins.

I heard more voices. Boys' piping tremelos, then the calls and whistles they employed to signal to one another.

Yodelling. Whistles.

Their bully lamps glowed in front of me.

How long did I follow them for?

The lanterns were constantly shifting position, dancing in the summer dark out there.

I continued running over the wet sand.

The bully lamps always kept ahead, obeying that same mysterious differential of distance, leading me on and on.

I was exhausted, yet I would have followed them anywhere.

And then suddenly ...

My legs folded beneath me, the strength was sapping out of them.

I found I was under water.

I flailed with my arms. Momentarily I made contact with the surface, I gulped at air. But a centrifugal energy was pulling me down and down. I was filled with a black terror, that I was now just about to die.

I had a headful of water. A vast blinding sandstorm blew.

Then two great palm trees appeared, and I was flying – flying over them and into them in slow motion. No, not palm trees, gigantic claw arms, the pincers of Cancer, seizing the little bits of me that were left. It was transporting the weight and mass I belonged to, through the wastes of time, past galaxies, past untold aeons of life and drowned planets.

A voice was calling across the heavens.

'Neil! Neil, can you hear me?'

I somersaulted through centuries, turned cartwheels across millennia.

'Wake up, Neil! Wake up!'

I came to. I came to with someone tugging at my shoulder.

Stars were ranged far, far above me.

I stared up into them. I was trying to remember.

I turned my head. My mother was sitting on the edge of the bed.

'What is it, son? What's happening to you? I don't understand.'

I couldn't speak, I could only shake my head at her.

'I can't help you, Neil. I *want* to help you.'

The centre light was on. I saw I had scratch marks on the backs of both hands, they were starting to bleed.

'Why can't you be like the old Neil, where's *he* gone?'

In those days, in that proudly self-reliant Presbyterian milieu of ours, no one would have countenanced giving time and presumed respect and – not least – hard-earned money to a psychiatrist.

Our sort gritted teeth and girded loins. If they absolutely had to, they lay low for a wee while and battened down the hatches.

What was it I was so frightened of not thinking about?

Something to do with what I'd only glimpsed that rainy night. The cars signalling with their headlights; the gleam of police uniforms; the commanding hand on the youth's arm; that single loud guffaw behind me, a manly knowing laugh, while I stood watching the pick-up outside the Central Hotel.

Nights were worst.

I would get up out of bed, stand upright to run the blood from my head, switch the ceiling light on. It was cold, so I walked about in my dressing-gown to keep warm. Around the small room, treading a constant circle of the square, with my transistor lead plugged into my ear to feed me pirate-radio pap.

Round and round.

My mother had given up going to church, 'putting in an appearance' as she used to call it.

'You sound disappointed, Neil.'

'No.' I shook my head. 'Not really.'

'There's nothing to stop *you* from going. If that's what you want to do.'

I shrugged. 'I don't know.'

189

'It doesn't mean I'm not a *Christian*.'

I heard the contending church bells of Kelvindale on Sunday mornings. I watched the worshippers hurrying off, men in their weekday suits and women in two-pieces and hats. Mentally I ran after them, I sneaked into the church at the back, squeezed into the gap left at the end of a pew, offered up an earnest prayer for the dead to rest in peace and leave the living with their life not to enjoy – God knows – but simply to bear.

My father asked to meet me in town.

He suggested a Ceylon Tea Centre close to the Central Hotel. I said, why not the Arts Galleries, two miles away in the opposite direction.

We shared a pot of tea there. Then we walked round, looking at the exhibits.

The dinosaur skeletons. The cases of stuffed winterland wildlife. The suits of armour. The scale models of Clyde-built ships, with their keels and propellers showing.

'Your mother and I both decided it was best like this.'

I didn't say anything.

'I thought you'd be old enough to cope with everything. Not a boy any more. Was I wrong?'

I shook my head.

'I hoped you'd be mature enough ...'

'I *am* mature enough.'

'Behaving how you've been behaving?'

'Mum's told you?'

'Is she wrong, Neil?'

'I don't know what she's said.'

'Not the half of it, I expect.'

I looked down at the floor.

'Your mother needs support. When I'm not there.'

'But you're not coming back.'

'Not to live, no. That's why she needs your support all the more.'

I stared over at the knight in his chain mail, visor closed, mounted on his armoured metal horse.

'I hoped you'd see that for yourself, Neil. I was depending on you. But if you feel you can't ...'

'I didn't say that.'

'I've always been very proud of you. Told everybody.'

I blinked hard.

'And then, I wondered if that Kildrennan business – .'

I talked over him.

'It's nothing. Nothing's wrong.'

'Your mother says – '

'It'll be all right. It'll be all right,' I said. 'You'll never have to mention it again.'

'No?'

'No.'

'You're sure?'

'I think we've seen everything in here.'

'Can you promise me, Neil?'

Of course I couldn't – but I did.

Everything was a lie, so what was one more?

My mother would study me over the top of her newspaper, or in the mirror.

On the good days she would smile to see me calmer, then shake out the newspaper and walk on past the mirror.

The bad days were better than they'd been, and she toughed them out, either at the kitchen cooker or sitting on the dressing-table stool darning my heels.

My father returned south, to an Air Force base in Lincolnshire. I had never been there, but I imagined the landscape: flat, damply green, a network of insignificant roads and drab little villages grimed in years of dust. Perhaps I was only guessing from the dismissive way my mother pronounced the names that appeared on the frank-marks on his letters, 'Spalding', 'Boston', 'Grantham'.

'He certainly gets around, Neil, doesn't he? Join the Air Force and see the world.'

In our day to day life, when there were just ourselves, she used more Scottish words than I remembered her using before Dad left. 'Wairsh', 'shilpit', 'wabbit', 'hirple', 'stravaig'. It was if she was erecting a wall of language around us, and further emphasising the fact of the man's exclusion by her ironic tone of voice each time she referred to 'your father's' this or that. She refused to call him 'Dad', as we'd both done in the old days, and even to her friends she spoke of 'Neil's father', not 'Eric' or 'my husband'.

191

She seemed to be trying to erase whatever evidence of him was left. She kept polishing the case of the wireless they'd bought when they got married – maybe to give her vengeful feelings another outlet – but she rubbed at it so hard that the wood veneer started to peel, right through to the chipboard beneath. She sent Dad back those books he'd neglected to take with him. She stopped smoking, really just so she could throw out the ashtrays. The double bed in her room was too expensive a purchase to change, but she covered the bedspread on the unused side with magazines, her sewing basket, a library book or two, a glass fruitbowl filled with hairgrips and rollers and nets.

I was forever expecting her to take up with, or be taken up by, another man. Now that she was working, in the youthful advertising agency, there were plenty of opportunities. It may have been that she was being very discreet about it, but if so I would surely have alighted on clues. Perhaps she intended to make a martyr of herself first: which was a dangerous course of action, since it isn't always possible to extricate oneself from that kind of self-justifying holiness. Still nobody appeared, and I realised how deeply her rancour went, to include the whole adult male sex. She couldn't forgive my father for having changed her, from the comely woman of my childhood whom other men might well have fallen for, into this weathered survivor, this hanger-on, needing to take pride in her so-called independence.

She started to speak sneerily of the English. In the past her criticisms had always been humorous ones. Now she mimicked their accents and scoffed at their colonialists' bad manners, their self-centredness, their insincerity, even their inability to cope with snow or floodwater. She dumped her disdain on to them by the shovel-load, which made Aunt Nessie's criticisms of the Sassenachs seem mild by comparison.

My father, I was made only too aware, wasn't going to be rehabilitated, not now, not a hope.

31

'Sing me a song of a lad that is gone', Stevenson wrote in his *Songs of Travel*. *'Say, could that lad be I?'*

The summer holidays were approaching.

For ten days in July, during the Fair break, my mother insisted I go on a school trip to Holland.

I told her I didn't want to go to Holland.

'Tell me something I don't know.'

'But I don't *want* – '

'You need a change of scene, Neil.'

'How d'you know that?'

'And I need a rest.'

She paid the cheque to the school.

'It's money I could've used for other things. But they'll have to wait. This is more important.'

'I didn't ask you to – '

'No one's going to say I'm a bad mother. That I didn't do the right thing.'

We had an earlier change of scene than anticipated.

Aunt Nessie had had an accident. She'd fallen and broken some bones in her leg. Nessie being Nessie, my mother said, we were only hearing about it after the worst was over. She'd been sent to recover in Auchendrennan's Cottage Hospital.

On the train my mother's eyes kept rising from her magazine to watch me across the compartment.

I felt increasingly agitated. I couldn't keep still. I bunched my right fist into my left hand, my left fist into my right hand.

The back of my shirt was wet and was sticking to the seat covering. I was aware of the big damp stains under my arms. My feet were hot inside my shoes. I wanted to scratch a persistent itch in the crack of my bottom.

The other passengers' chatter, about nothing, irritated me so much I had to get up, I blundered past them into the corridor. I pulled the window down in the door, to cool my face. I breathed in the smoke that trailed past, and I smelt the smell from last time, the journey down at the end of the previous June.

I locked myself in the toilet. I stared into the mirror. I had a wolf in my face.

Cold, hunted eyes.

I threw water over my cheeks, my brow, I watched it trickle from my chin – my muzzle – back into the basin.

Under my breath I spoke all the foulest words I could think of. No one could have heard as the carriage shook around me, axles juddered, the wheels whined on the tracks.

I reached out and touched the cold glass of the mirror. The wolf stared back from its frozen floe country.

Greyness. Old stone. The dull clamour of history. Wind turning on the street corners.

The mounting block. The iron jougs.

They were still here. Nothing had gone away.

I walked into my old bedroom. My stomach turned over, smelling it again: the sachet of spiced petal husks hanging from the hook on the back of the door, the oozy candlewick bedspread. I pictured the darkness beneath the floorboards. I ran a finger through the dust on top of the dressing-table. The view from the window was like an ache to me.

The hunched bungalows in their dry gardens. Sand blown inland, amassed under privet and holly hedges. Washing pegged out on back greens. A rug being beaten with a cane switch. Polished curling stones, on front steps swept two or three times a day.

I had hardly given a thought to Aunt Nessie as an invalid, except to imagine her splayed out in traction.

But we found her in the Cottage Hospital sitting up in a chair, with her right leg and hip encased in plaster.

I seemed to embarrass her. She kept pulling her lacy dressing gown tighter about her, while I made a show of diverting my eyes away.

'A proper ass I've gone and made of myself.'

194

'Not at all.' My mother patted her arm.

'I'd laugh, I think. If it wasn't so painful.'

'Poor Nessie!'

'Poor you. And Neil too, of course.'

'We're here to make things easier for you.'

Aunt Nessie returned my mother's condolent expression with one of her own, for what my mother had gone through – might still be going through.

I couldn't get to sleep.

I lay watching last summer pass across the ceiling. I remembered all the feelings I'd had lying in this bed then.

I closed my eyes, but I still saw the same pictures. I opened them again and turned to the wall, but they were there too, unmistakable like watermarks through the paper's fussy pattern of pergola bowers.

My mother would shade her eyes with her hand and gaze out at the bay for minutes on end, filling her head with the thrill of the light and the receding planes of distance.

She was losing her Glasgow pallor. Her posture had changed; she'd lost the defensive set of her shoulders, and forgot to be a coiled spring.

In the chemist's she bought a new compact. She would take the felt sheath from her bag, slide out the compact, and study herself in the mirror in the circular lid; she didn't frown at what she saw, and even though she used two fingers to try pressing out the grooves etched into her brow above the nose, astragal lines, she seemed happier with the person she closed inside the compact, flicking the lid up at the very last moment for a final check, as if she was superstitious about not finding her there the next time.

We'd gone into The Girnel tea-rooms.

'To get us out of the house,' my mother said. And away from the stuffy atmosphere of the Cottage Hospital.

None of Aunt Nessie's friends was in, so my mother had some respite. She eased, and even indulged in a cigarette.

For me there was no respite, no possibility of settling at all. My mouth was parched, so I gulped the hot tea down, but I couldn't have eaten. My mother was saved the price of two cakes therefore, which left her even better disposed, protracting the pleasure of her own almond slice with

195

white icing. The windows were starting to steam up, and the view was disappearing, which made me feel more claustrophobic than ever. I noticed some of the voices roundabout had been lowered, in that show of discretion which hints that confidences or criticisms are being traded.

At last we were ready to leave. I reached the door first while my mother, still buoyant, went back to place a small minding for the waitress under the saucer of her cup. The door didn't open easily, and I pulled harder the second time, which had the bells jangling merry hell.

I stepped outside. The first face I saw walking towards me was Maitland's.

We both stopped and stared.

After a couple of seconds he turned his head away and continued walking.

No other acknowledgement was made.

In those two seconds his face had revealed a succession of emotions as the blood drained away.

Disbelief. Rancour. And a kind of terror too.

Some of his hair was quite a different colour. He hadn't thought to use the bottle of dye, meant to restore the grey to black. The trauma of events had turned half the grey to white.

I stood and watched him walk off. I felt myself shaking. I had thought I might avoid him – Maitland wasn't a man for walking about the town streets.

'Neil – '

I jumped at my mother's voice.

' – did you think I'd got lost?'

She smiled in a puzzled way.

'You look as if someone's just walked on your grave. What is it?'

I shook my head.

'Well, don't go spoiling our nice afternoon.'

'I'm sorry,' I said.

'So you should be. Giving me a turn like that.'

I knew where the cemetery was.

I had to go in past the caretaker's lodge. It was the same wall-eyed man, watching me over the yellowed net at his window.

I took several minutes to find the grave. I presumed it would be somewhere by itself. There was some space left, about a lair wide, on either

196

side, but beyond that the deceased burghers of Auchendrennan crowded round, just as presumptuous in death as in life, with their draped urns and harpist angels and Celtic crosses.

Bone's headstone was singularly plain. An unadorned rectangle of black slate. His names 'Euan Andrew Gault Bone' and two dates '1925-1963' and a quotation, which I later tracked down to Stevenson, a poem called 'Youth and Travel' in *Songs of Travel*.

The untented Kosmos my abode,
I pass, a wilful stranger

No Christian exhortation. Nothing else, except some dried bird droppings on the slate.

I turned and ran.

As I was leaving by the main gates, on to the back road up from the town, I heard a car starting up, a plump sportif revving. I saw it from behind, driving off. The white and blue Facel. It had almost reached the corner, taking the bend too fast, turning old leaves out of the unkempt verge and spinning them.

From the harbour my eyes kept returning to the high white walls and the turret of Slezer's Wark.

I saw bonfire smoke from the garden, rising behind the sea wall. Life went on, the garden still had to be attended to, routines had to be kept up.

Autumn was the season for bonfires. But for Maitland the seasons must have been knocked out of kilter. The gardener was doing no more than making up now. A signal was going, that nature didn't wait, it made no concessions.

I heard a car behind me. The engine purred, the tyres hissed softly on the tarmac.

An expensive marque, I could tell.

The road curved. I turned my head, looked out of the corner of my eye.

The car, with white about its bodywork, continued to follow me.

I didn't know what to do. Keep on walking? Stop still? Or try to get away, make a run for it – ?

Events overtook me. The Facel drew alongside. The driver's window was wound down. Maitland was staring over at me.

I watched him as I walked on. His eyes didn't even blink, he was transfixed. He was unhinged maybe.

197

All the past came roaring back at me.

He was wanting to ask me, what happened? How could it have happened like that? What is it you're not allowing yourself to think about – ?

He didn't ask me anything. He couldn't speak.

The car was keeping pace with me. I continued walking, even though I felt I was crawling on my knees. The muscles in my legs weren't working. Keep walking, Pritchard – somehow, just keep walking …

The car started to move ahead of me, I fell behind. The engine sounded more assertive on the incline.

Nothing had been said. But words weren't necessary. His haunted stare had spoken for him: and for me, my anxiety not to stop.

I felt that, coming so close to Aunt Nessie's life and yet discovering so little about her, my mother was envious.

She envied her the capacity to keep secrets. She had elected to lead her life more positively, with a husband and child; her own secrets had become watered down, so that she wouldn't feel guilty about them, which wasn't the point of secrets, and so she'd gradually surrendered most of them, as being impractical to a wife and mother who prided herself on her efficiency.

I saw another bonfire, another trail of smoke from behind the sea wall of Slezer's Wark.

Against the house's high white walls the smoke curled darkly.

The fire continued to be stoked.

The task, whatever it was, was well in hand.

I waited until nightfall, until I could see from the shore that the fire had gone out.

The gates on to the street were open and I went in, running from shadow to shadow. The garage doors were pulled shut. A few lights were on in the house, upstairs.

I smelt out where the bonfire had been burning. The ground had been scorched.

I raked among the cool ashes with my hands. The moon was up already, and I looked for any pieces of paper that showed white. On some I could just make out the tracks of a fountain pen, phrases from several sentences. I fanned my hands and delved beneath, through the layers of burnt paper, to find anything that was merely charred on its edges.

I placed my finds, my jetsam, on one side carefully, respectfully: these relics of the past now rescued from oblivion.

★

Maitland had destroyed Bone's diary, it was to transpire.

Most of the working papers he left, because they were too disorganised and because they didn't directly relate to their personal life together.

All the letters between them must have gone up in flames too.

I knew Bone's handwriting.

> *hat's dome is done & won't ev*
> *epeated. I've put you through*
> *itterly regret all that's happe*
> *serve much better, Christ kno*
> *& put it to the back of our min*
> *arry on as we mean to contin*

At Skerryvore I tested the floor, located that one squeaky board. I shifted my weight on it, and it creaked.

I left what I knew was beneath just where it was, where it now belonged, in the darkness and dust.

> *n tell you in the music how I*
> *ifference it's made to everyth*
> *ou'll hear what no one else wil*
> *ldn't have written any of it witho*
> *nly way I know to tell you just how*
> *nd listen to it not as anyone else is g*
> *r ears but in yr heart also. My darling Dou*
> *he best repayment I can hope to give yo*

Part Five

32

I'm walking down a dark street late at night. A couple of fitful streetlights show me the way.

It's a street with cobbles, and tramlines still in place.

It's years ago now. But I can hear voices, I follow the sounds. Laughter, arguments. Lights spill out through frosted glass on to the pavement at the far corner, leaving a greasy sheen.

I want to reach the corner, to get ahead of myself so that I can stop whatever is going to happen from happening. But my legs won't function properly, and now I'm weighted to the spot.

What's holding me back?

Fear, loathing, disgust. Take your pick.

Bone and Maitland were to miss out on swinging London.

They didn't even get to taste the new decade in the capital.

For the times, though – the mid '50s – London was the best place to be, and they made the most of it, in the supperclubs and cocktail bars, in the blue-lit restricted access rooms at the backs of private men-only clubs.

They each encouraged the other to become what they hadn't been to begin with, increasingly cosmopolitan sophisticates.

Forays were made down to Bournemouth. There on the piney avenues, among the green-roofed villas and mansion blocks with porterage, they rendezvoused with friends. In the deep wooded chines that run down to the sea they went to seek out strangers, a rougher sort, who shared the same physical wants as themselves.

It had always been called the Blue House.

The exterior walls were painted blue, and they continued the tradition after Maitland had bought the property and they'd moved in. A lighter cerulean blue this time, instead of the royal blue of the previous owner.

It could be seen from the other side of the Heath. Blue walls: and white shutters at the windows. At a distance the windows would seem wide-awake or appear to be winking, or asleep behind closed eyelids. In the garden, cedar trees with their flat branches, like plate-stands. Views down-hill of the vast sprawl of London.

The unmade road outside the Blue House would fill with cars on party evenings or for the Sunday brunches or for the faux-Proustian salons which took place on Bank Holidays, when the rest of the population was disporting itself vulgarly.

★

[From a taped interview, London 21 September 1997
C.S., originally a home news journalist on a Fleet Street daily]
In those days – '56, '57 – I had a contact in Scotland Yard, my copy-buddy. Other news hacks in London, like me, they had theirs too. Each of us, we guarded the relationship we had.

I heard about Bone – Bone and Maitland – but it was one of those dead stories – I mean, you couldn't use it, it didn't even get as far as the newsroom spike – they'd have guessed where it came from. Anyway, someone higher up at the Yard – tarred with their brush, maybe a music lover too – he'd covered the tracks over very nicely.

I knew what I knew. But that was as far as it went, or as far as I could take it, I couldn't start running with it anywhere else.

The boy – called Simon – had been singing for Bone, every afternoon up at the Blue House. The music was being set to lyrics in Middle Scots, to narrate incidents in the life of Scotland's first major composer, Robert Carver, four hundred years ago.

The boy belonged to a cathedral choir, and knew to be disciplined. Work went well. Bone felt inspired, up on the healthful Heath.

Then disaster struck. The boy's voice cracked, with the cantata no more than half-completed. They struggled on. But Bone and the boy (not technically a boy any longer) both realised it was useless.

The daily arrangement ceased.

Bone tried to continue without him. Then it occurred to him, if he at least maintained contact with Simon, the flow of inspiration might return.

Maitland wasn't so sure. Bone met the lad without telling Maitland, although Maitland subsequently discovered. It was a different sort of relationship now. Bone took the boy to cafés, they went swimming in the weedy ponds hidden about the Heath, where they bathed naked.

Maitland came home one afternoon and his eye alighted on fresh semen stains on the stair carpet.

The boys' parents, alerted by the Charterhouse staff that he was regularly missing classes, had had him followed. They contacted the police.

Two officers and a back-up constable called at the Blue House. Bone and Maitland were both taken in for questioning. Maitland was sent home, but Bone remained in custody for further questioning. The interrogation lasted on and off for forty hours. Bone was released.

He was accompanied back to the Blue House. It was explained to him and Maitland by a senior inspector that charges would not be pressed if both men left London forthwith and did not return.

By leaving London, it was understood that they were to leave England. The inspector acknowledged that pleas had been received on Bone's behalf from a number of famous names in the musical firmament; he was willing to accede to their requests, that Bone should be allowed to work on, but it must be out of the ken of his own or any English police force. On Bone's part there must be no, repeat no, attempt to return. And the inspector advised against any further communication with the minor who had been interfered with. He hoped that he would hear of neither man again 'except in an artistic capacity'.

Maitland's position wasn't so clear. Some guilt attached to him by association. He did venture back to London a couple of times, just briefly, for bravura's sake perhaps. But he passed into the background more easily, even in the early '60s there were lots of older tweedy types from the shires still about. (All those sexy young aristos in the pages of *Queen*, forgiven their class, looking for a piece of the action.)

Bone kept his distance. He must have been tempted. But in Galloway he was able to get his music written, there were compensations.

It took an urbane sense of irony to switch to linen trousers and sandals and smock-shirts.

Auchendrennan wouldn't be the same, Bone was advertising to Maitland and to their friends. Slezer's Wark looked like nothing in London. The interior mapped a private world: bits of London, but also bits of Scotland, bits of Italy, furniture and fittings with a provenance ranging from the West Indies (that cromandel hall chair with the shell back made on site for a sugar plantation house) to Muslim Russia (the bokhara floor-runners).

By some fluke, a rough notebook of Carver material escaped Maitland's notice and survived the bonfires.

Chantour Full Cheif in the Cannonry
The Merciment of Fire
Ring Song
Echo Repercust

Various dates in the margins confirm that Carver – whether a cantata or really an opera in embryo – was being worked on during the last ten months of residence at the Blue House.

4 Part Mass	*Pater Creator Omnium*
	L'Homme Arme
5 Part Mass	*Fera persima*
10 Part Mass	*Dum sacrum mysterium*
2 Motets	*Gaude flore virginali (5-parts)*
	O bone Jesu (19-parts)

Like The Lantern Bearers, Carver was being led by a voice, Simon's – the inspiration of the music that had been unleashed over the winter and spring, not like any other, but abruptly checked by the cruel machinations of the boy's biology.

If there had been a religious impulse to begin with, it was lost in all the brouhaha that followed, leading to the exile.

In Auchendrennan Bone read a book of Stevenson's essays, which included 'The Lantern Bearers'.

And then, in the course of that summer of 1962, I chanced to come along.

Maitland understood what the dangers were in my being there, at Slezer's Wark.

To Bone, because of the past. And to myself, because I was a muddle-headed mixture of knowingness and ignorance.

He also understood that I was essential to Bone's project, and so to domestic harmony in Slezer's Wark.

He wanted to protect Bone, and that meant protecting me also.

Earlier than either Bone or myself, he had sought to limit the damage. I shouldn't grow too fond of Slezer's Wark, and Bone shouldn't imagine he was too dependent on me.

In the days coming after my expulsion, I thought I had the evidence against Maitland, but in reality it was a different sort of proof, which I couldn't read.

33

t how can I make you believ
the truth, nothing but the tru
gree that it's asking you to trust
fter this length of time that you kno
othing should ever be allowed to com
ldn't bear to think that anything migh
be sadder than I could poss. put into wor

1970.

Tiles had blown off the roof of Slezer's Wark. Some had crashed into the cold frames in the garden. The walls, once famously white, had been dirtied by the weather. The windows carried a crust of sea salt.

The garden hadn't been tended for five or six years. The beds were overgrown, choked with weeds. The leaves and fallen fruit from past seasons lay uncollected and rotting in the long grass.

No one came in any more to clean or cook. There was nobody to tell what sort of state the house was like inside. A doctor was summoned once in a while, but elderly Dr Joss was the curmudgeonly soul of discretion. The telephone had needed to be repaired, and an engineer was called in, who talked afterwards of bad smells and old newspapers on the floors to cover puddles, but he wouldn't say any more than that. (Had he been paid for his silence?) Sometimes boys from the town dared one another to look in through the grimy windows.

Small regular grocery orders were delivered and left in an outhouse for Maitland; to judge from the little that was supplied every week he must have eaten very sparely, like a mouse. He received mail, but sent out hardly anything, leaving whatever it was for the trusted delivery man from Leckie's to post for him.

Slezer's Wark used to be considered one of the town's sights. Now it was thought to be an unlucky spot. The locals didn't linger nearby, they hurried past. The high building, with its stepped corbie-stanes and round-topped turret, sent longer shadows across the street, and they seemed somehow colder than other shadows. It was the house in a dark adventure story, one by Robert Louis Stevenson perhaps, it was the gaunt and lowering House of Shaws.

Various members of the Maitland family had troubled themselves to make the journey to the coast, to try to talk sense into this most wayward scion of the clan. But, as Mrs Faichnie put about, to no avail. Maitland resisted them all, even his redoubtable older sister, the 'BV'.

> *ut don't know what to say &*
> *pologise aren't going to be enoug*
> *n time p'haps we'll get a perspec*
> *ll fall into their proper place. That'*
> *my earnest hope in the meanti*
> *nd mull it over and try to grant*
> *or asking you to judge against yo*
> *f you can find it in you to forgi*
> *o time will tell the best way to g*

Maitland was to die of pneumonia.

His body lay in the house for two weeks before the alarm was raised.

He was found wearing soiled pyjamas and a ripped or shredded dressing-gown.

He had lost several stones in weight.

On the kitchen floor empty wine and spirits bottles were lined up with the precision of a military file, and they almost ringed the room.

All the photographs in their silver or tortoiseshell frames had vanished a long while ago.

The electric radiogram was switched on, and now red-hot to the touch. It was playing a record on repeat, one of himself playing a composition by Bone dedicated to him. The record had been spinning for a fortnight; the stylus was worn down, and the music was almost unrecognisable, smoothed and smoothed away back into the vinyl and scarcely audible.

A search of the house revealed that nothing at all remained of their private correspondence.

Maitland had been careful with the music. Two complete and unpublished pieces by Bone were found, and a drawerful of rejected work and juvenilia. Also, a number of items in progress at the time Bone died.

But not a trace of The Lantern Bearers.

Another drawer contained Bone's work books; pages which might have referred to sources of which Maitland didn't approve had been torn out.

Maitland had anticipated the interest there would be one day. He had also been jealous enough to want to exclude others from the story of their lives. There was nobody else, only Bone and himself, and the details of their relationship must remain concealed and intensely private.

From so little corroborating matter, legends are more easily made.

> *can't tell yo*
> *means to me tha*
> *nd say these things to*
> *ow you love me. Deares*

Maitland was buried beside Bone.

Bone's memorial stone stood upright. Maitland had opted for one lain flat, but of the same black slate. It carried two dates '1911–1970' and three more lines from Stevenson.

> *Under the wide and starry sky*
> *Dig the grave and let me lie*
> *Glad did I live and gladly die*

34

– Mr Duggan?

– Speaking.

– Excuse me ringing.

– Who is this?

– I was able to get hold of your number.

– Who are you?

– My name's Pritchard. Neil Pritchard.

– Who?

– Eric Pritchard's son.

– Eric Pritchard? The Lodge. Yes.

– You remember – the Euan Bone business?

– I … I remember.

– I was wondering if I could ask –

– But I don't discuss specific cases. I'm retired now.

– It can't *matter* now, though, can it? After thirty-something years –

– What can't matter?

– I don't know. Offending sensibilities.

– I see.

– Betraying confidences.

– 'Betraying'? Why d'you choose that word?

– I have to know what happened. Why Bone died.

– 'Why'?

– *How*, then.

– No, I'm sorry, Mr Pritchard.

– What are you hiding?

– What am *I* hiding? We acted on your initiative, if I'm not mistaken.

– Bone died.

– Yes, Mr Pritchard.

– He died or he was killed.

– His death has long been a matter of regret to me.

– You had no idea what a risk you were taking? Using ruffians like that – ?

– I need to ask, Mr Pritchard – did *you* calculate the risks?

– I was a boy.

– Evidently you knew a lot about the world.

– No, I didn't.

– According to your father.

– All that stuff …

– It was true, what you told him?

– I …

– It *wasn't* true, what you told him?

– The news reports didn't say what had happened to Bone. Not what *really* happened. How he died. If he was dead before you could get him back to the hotel, smuggled him in –

– Those are your theses, are they?

– Why won't you say? 'Yea' or 'nay'. Why won't you come clean?

– Tell me, Mr Pritchard. How far back in the story would your news sleuths have had to go. Eh? Would they have had to bring your father in? And you?

I'm sorry. I feel this conversation – it isn't going to get us anywhere.

– End of story? Is it?

– Why are you asking me these things now, Mr Pritchard?

– Let sleeping dogs lie? You'd prefer that?

– I'd prefer? I'm trying to save the situation.

– 'Save it'? Why're you trying to –

– For conscience's sake, shall we say?

– Is that guilt speaking, Mr Duggan? Inspector Duggan? Guilt – at last?

– No, no. I am considering your own conscience, Mr Pritchard. Your own peace of mind. Believe me.

Now, if you'll excuse me –

– But I haven't asked –

– I'm ex-directory, Mr Pritchard. You did well to find me. But I should appreciate if we could regard this as our last word –

– But you're the only person I can ask.

– Goodnight, Mr Pritchard. My regards to your parents.

– My father died last year.

– I'm sorry to hear that. I didn't know. But you must excuse me now – …

★

212

The One-o-One restaurant in Hope Street has gone, and its swirly Hollywood-ish elegance with it; it was replaced long ago by, of all things, a bookmakers'.

The Central Hotel survives, but dimmed. The original proprietors were British Railways, who brought style and glamour to each of their three stately station hotels in Glasgow.

The city centre still holds to the grid template of streets. Some of the more Gothic red sandstone edifices have been demolished, replaced first by '70s and '80s office buildings, and those replaced in their turn in the '90s. But enough is left for me to realise that I'm in the same place, with surprise vistas down long straight side-lanes between the sandstone or mirror-plated blocks, with the sculpted caryatids and ancient heroes – Classical or Scots – still occupying their niches storeys up at roof level. The sandstone has been blasted clean, and the pigeons and starlings are fewer than they were, and I miss the grimy chiaroscuro of soot-stained walls and the shrill vocalising of the birds perched on wires like crotchets and semiquavers.

★

A couple of weeks after my telephone conversation with Inspector Duggan as was, I received a police file, sent anonymously.

It came from the Glasgow records, 1959-1963.

'MAITLAND / BONE'.

It had been sealed shortly after Bone's death.

Any information concerning their London sojourn had been removed. The enclosures referred to their political sympathies and affiliations.

A nationalist cell was active in Central Scotland, only a few years after the last had been rooted out. Maitland and Bone were known to be acquainted with a couple of its leading lights; several academics in Glasgow and Edinburgh had gathered an intellectual clique which offered moral support to the 'field troops'. It was strongly suspected that Maitland had also provided funds for the agitators' endeavours.

There followed a record of the pair's movements, a list of sightings, statements from witnesses and interested parties either denying or confirm-ing the involvement of the two men.

Reading between the lines of the confidential reports, it was the pair's

213

high profile – especially Bone's – which was proving the difficulty. Any evidence collected had to be surefire, watertight.

The file also included mention of myself, and my statement to my father as reported to Inspector Duggan, King Street. The language was formal and impersonal; although details weren't any more specific than 'a wood', 'the bathroom', 'EB's bedroom', the nature of my accusation was quite clear and unambiguous.

The two men's nationalism probably owed less to affection for Scotland than to their continuing anger at being denied a life in England.

Just as I was banished from Slezer's Wark, so they had been banished from the Blue House on the Heath.

Their resentment had grown no less. After six years they felt just as strongly, that they had been conspired against; they'd been less at fault than those who – with Scotland Yard's full complicity – had hounded them out. London was where they had wanted to be; they'd made it there, all the way up to the top of the the hill – and then, in no more than the forty-eight hours granted them, they'd had to pack and and take their leave.

The file had lost its buff colouring along the top edge, faded by the sun in some exposed office location.

The paper had yellowed, and the typewriter ink faded.

Isn't it all history now? Duggan was asking me. But don't let me think him obstructive. Anyway, I was surely too much implicated to want to advertise my part in the tragedy.

He was taking no responsibility for what had happened.

*

What did happen?
Something like this maybe.

The things I'd told my father provided Duggan and his colleagues with an excuse to move in on Bone, to – literally – apply some pressure.

Maitland was their chief quarry, but Bone would be the means of exerting some emotional leverage on him.

A young parole prisoner was given his orders; he proved to be the tasty bit of bait.

Bone was persuaded perhaps by the youth's mentioning Maitland: a message was waiting for him – if he'd only come with him, it wasn't far, just a few blocks, down near the river.

There had been some (rehearsed) horseplay inside the pub. And as Bone tried to get away it spilled outside (as arranged) into the lane at the back.

A handpush or two, a slap.

The police had given them their instructions, what to ask.

Tell us what you know. Who're these Nat bastards? What's your sugar daddy got to do with them? C'mon, we want some *names*. The fuck you don't know. Name names, man!

Another handpush or two, a little more spirited; another slap, a degree rougher.

Bone lost his balance, let's say, he fell. Knocked his head against the wall, or the kerb, or the cobbles.

It could have happened very easily, and very suddenly. Everyone – Bone included, quite possibly – would have been fuelled by alcohol. In the dark it would have been hard to see, wouldn't it?

The death certificate ascribed the fatality to 'cardiac arrest'.

There is no hospital record extant to provide an account of events. No mention anywhere of a Casualty patient that night, one Euan Bone.

The newspapers of the time didn't voice any suspicions, or didn't dare to.

Some of Bone's friends thought heart failure was a convenient catch-all verdict. They knew he'd been very badly bruised and bleeding profusely, internally and externally. Did pains in his chest presage the fall, or did the fall precipitate a heart attack? How much harm had been done to him getting him back to the Central Hotel from the back lane behind the pub? Or was he already dead before they could lift him up from the wet cobbles?

Long ago my mind blotted out what had happened. What must have happened.

Shades of black. The very blackest was what I could never reveal to myself – my involvement. Around it by degrees, the panoply of dreams and superstitions.

I didn't forget. The very opposite was true: I was failing to remember, precisely because I refused to let myself think about it. I couldn't live with knowing what I knew, so I painted it out. Blackness blacks out everything.

35

I came over from Italy in 1995 when my mother sent me the telegram.

I said I would travel to Auchendrennan alone, ahead of my mother, to arrange Aunt Nessie's funeral.

There was another matter I had to attend to as well.

On my first sight of the town from the train, I closed my eyes.

When I opened them again, it was still there.

A closed town. A sleeping dog of a place with head touching tail.

Grey on grey.

Just the same. Any differences were unimportant ones.

A new building on the station concourse with crinkly plastic vandal-proof windows instead of glass. A burger-bar at the far corner, instead of the old tea-room with steaming urn.

Crossing the concourse, I noticed a youth emerging from the tiled doorway of the Gents'. He walked straight towards me.

'Got a light, pal?'

He held a cigarette between index and second fingers. His thumb flicked the coloured tip, and the cigarette rose to a 60-degree angle.

Was I so easy to spot?

'Sorry,' I said. I tried to move past him.

'Thought I could ask *you*.'

He had hard angry eyes.

'I'm sorry,' I told him.

'Fucking piss off!'

But he let me go, and I walked away quickly. Thirty years ago it wouldn't have happened like this, not in Auchendrennan. Now drugs came into sexual transactions, just as much in a backwater town as in a city.

Tempora mutantur. Indeed.

I got the last taxi. I asked for Hauselock Avenue.

'You know the town?'

'Haven't been here since I was a boy,' I told the driver.

He was about my own age. Brylcreemed red hair, a stab at a quiff, a bushy red moustache. Whey unsunned skin, and a double chin.

'Will you be wanting the scenic route?'

I shrugged. 'What's the difference?'

'About three quid.'

I looked at my watch.

'Another time,' I said. 'I want to get there while it's light.'

I realised just how much I hadn't wanted to see the town again. I only wished to get this business over and done with.

My red-haired driver started singing quietly to the country-and-western tune on the radio.

Aunt Nessie's bungalow had changed hardly at all in thirty years, since I was last in it. I imagined I could smell three decades' worth of time accumulated in the airless rooms.

I found things as my aunt had left them when she'd had her first stroke. A *Woman and Home* which had slithered down the side of her chair beside the fire. A cup of tea where her neighbour who'd come in to clear up hadn't thought to look, on the under-shelf of the little table; the rancid milk had turned the tea blue.

The rooms were silent, except whenever I stood on a rogue floorboard. The clocks had stopped; I remembered how the plumbing pipes behind the walls used to gurgle and, on bath nights, judder.

I could hear the blood pounding inside my head.

Poor Aunt Nessie. With all that blood exploding inside her chest.

I sat down at the kitchen table. Some underwear still hung on the pulley. How she would have hated me seeing that.

I looked over at the window. It was the same view I'd gazed out at for the weeks of that summer. The green-painted iron poles she'd hitched her washing-line to, a rowan tree, the fir beyond, and the unevenly cut yellow privet hedge. Not part of the original view was the top of a conservatory someone had added to another bungalow. But that apart, I was seeing just what I'd seen at fourteen years old.

From the hotel I rang Alec in Rome.

I asked him how the cats were, what he'd been doing with himself. Whether he'd been able to fix dinner with Ben and Michael.

I told him I loved him, I wished I could go to bed with him, right now. Once I'd put the phone down I realised why it had been important to say that, with so much clarity, so he should never misunderstand me.

Since Maitland's death the Bone industry had developed in earnest.

Concerts, recordings. Monographs, articles, a radio feature followed by a television documentary. An exhibition of photographs which transferred to London. The first biography, followed by a second.

The festival in Auchendrennan was no longer biennial but annual. When the chance presented itself, the festival committee had bid for Slezer's Wark; restored to its original glory, it now accommodated the Bone-Maitland Study Centre.

Auchendrennan prospered from the connection. Performances took place in any half-suitable venue. There was a Crotchets coffee shop. You could buy Auchendrennan Festival t-shirts and pottery mugs. The small hotels and guest-houses were busy at selected intervals throughout the year.

Some vocal townsfolk complained, as the Scots always do, but Auchendrennan if not wholly proud of the association was comfortably reconciled to it.

I rolled back the carpet and underfelt in my old bedroom. Beetles scampered out.

I loosened the floorboard and prised it up at one end.

A cold draught blew up into my face, and dust, and more of that stink of old time.

I waited a few moments before I reached in and felt about with my hand.

At first I couldn't find anything. I panicked. My heart was banging against my ribs.

Then my fingers brushed against – what? Paper.

Papers, plural. They felt soft and damp.

I pulled them out.

The rubber band must have perished, the sheets were loose.

Very carefully I unrolled the pages, blowing the dirt off them. The notes and the words were still legible.

I sank back on my heels and closed my eyes with relief.

Bone was doing a roaring trade. A Euan Bone season on BBC Radio 3, at the Proms, an Omnibus to come on TV.

But, in CritSpeak, there was one piece missing from the jigsaw.

Whatever happened to The Lantern Bearers?

According to friends and colleagues, it was the one work of his last two years which Bone regarded with some pride. They'd been allowed to hear snatches of it, and could believe it would have been one of his finest achievements.

It must have been accidentally lost when Maitland destroyed the private correspondence. Maitland had always been the staunchest advocate of Bone's music; even sunk in his long last depression would he have contemplated diminishing Bone's posthumous reputation?

Only I knew the likely answer.

After his sighting of me outside The Girnel tea-rooms that afternoon, it must have been Maitland's consuming need to destroy every last trace and vestige of Neil Pritchard's time at Slezer's Wark.

I sat into the night with my copy of the manuscript.

Two hours, three hours.

Memories kept intervening.

But I also felt I was understanding the music properly for the first time. How Bone had put it together, the secondary musical themes submerged beneath the vocal top lines. The processes of his mind from page to page, from one verbal picture to the next. The counterpointing.

I was a man older than Bone when he wrote it. Perhaps I had never felt closer to Bone than I did at two o'clock on this September morning, in the silence of the avenues.

36

I've been asked more and more to write about Euan Bone.
It's thought that I have a particular 'empathy' with his music.

In the newly devolved Scotland, Bone is turning into a cultural icon, in the rushed search to find heroes. The attention is deserved. The music speaks for itself, even if the biographical information – what might be gleaned from letters and diaries – is severely depleted in Bone's case.
Until now.
In putting the record straight about the final months of Bone's short life I must help to annihilate myself. But that process, as the specialist's X-rays told me, is already well under way.

The authenticity of my account will be debated.
I've proved myself a fantasist at one point already, with the direst consequences. Perhaps I'm only telling stories now?
Might be.
But why should I crucify myself like this, and do the two men to death again, for anything less than the truth?
The music is my proof.

I'm in one of those high-drama Hollywood films Bone and Maitland and the Slezer's Wark set used to laugh about but which they watched to help exorcise deeper feelings and fears in themselves.
Thirty months to live. Two years if I'm fortunate.
Nothing concentrates the mind so ably as a sense of the inevitable. Even the horror subsides, and a bizarre fearlessness takes over.

★

I took a last look at the Blue House. Then I went back to the car, started the engine, lifted the handbrake. I followed the signs to take me back down into town.

Traffic headlights coming uphill towards me dazzled through the dust on the windscreen. All I could see were the lights – in a smir of blown sand – luring me.

'... the slide shut, the top-coat buttoned: not a ray escaping, whether to conduct your footsteps or to make your glory public'.

I had been here before. A house, moving lights, confusion massing in the air at the end of the day. This regret, and the uncontainable longing. What might be said, and what couldn't be.

'... and all the while, deep down in the privacy of your fool's heart, to know you had a bull's-eye at your belt, and to exult and sing over the knowledge.'

Another café, a brasserie. Old Compton Street. The pink pound.

Hungry glances. Gym-honed shoulder bumping against shoulder, the backs of hands and knuckles touching, little fingers entwining.

Car tyres sizzle on the dry street as they glide past. Restless cruising eyes are turning in every direction.

And in another year and a half I might be dead. Somehow I have to make the time count, every single minute of it. I have to free myself of everything that I can extricate myself from. There'll be enough to cope with, simply surviving.

Atonement, redemption, mercy ... they're just words, to the godless like me. But equally words are all I have, and my best hope to clearing my mind.

★

The work to Bone – and to Maitland – was paramount, sovereign.

Its creation was both fire and ice. The grandeur of heaven, and its infinite incomprehensibility.

' "Beware the heat o' the sun".'

Bone burned us all up. He demanded us, and consumed us, and – mysteriously – the music excuses everything.

★

Paul Quigley has gone on to enjoy a distinguished career. He has a special affinity with Bone's music; using advanced digital sound, he has

221

recorded all the pieces that were written for Douglas Maitland and dedi-.
cated to him.

's too precious to allow oursel
eopardising the future for the sak
nimportant compared with what we
romise that I shall never betray past c
give you my solemn word on it, so help
ou'll never again need to doubt my inten
it behind us and get on with life together,

But even those high definition 24-bit recordings of Bone's cello pieces
– plus some of the repertoire pieces of other composers which Maitland was
known for – haven't superseded the original '50s and early '60s recordings.

In Maitland's versions, partly because the microphone is closer, you hear
the fingering more clearly, a few strains and stumbles, even the sound of
the man's breathing, little catches of air and excitement in his throat. He is
nearer us, and the music seems nearer to its making, more vital and more
necessary.

All Quigley's faultless technique, and the smooth meticulous shiny
recordings, can't convince us what the music once meant – to Bone, who
was expressing his private feelings for the man, and to Maitland, for whose
idiosyncracies of playing it was tailored and who would be the first to lift
his bow to the strings and give the music sound.

★

Glasgow.

These too.

The street down to the Clyde has been re-developed, in the spirit of Old
Compton Street.

Clothes shops. A wine bar. A small chi-chi hotel. A dance club called
Boyz Room.

Everything has a gay intonation. Cloneville.

The pub on the corner is now an arcade of five boutiques. More clothes,
books, a pâtisserie, a tanning-studio. It's the same if you're there at 3pm or
3am, you will be among your own kind and as safe as you might be
anywhere else, perhaps more so.

But it's not the street I continue to walk down, where I stand on the opposite pavement by a lamppost that's on the blink, watching and waiting. On that street the air smells not of after-shave and spray-on pâtisserie 'atmosphere'; it smells of the river, a tang of salt and iodine, and of foreign journeys, and menace unseen.

37

It's now a daily grind of sessions at the clinic and work on 'Bone' and sickness and sly suspicions.

On the wall in front of my desk I've stuck two lines of John Berryman.
> Write as short as you can,
> In order, of what matters.

Next to it, the label for a wine bottle, with its colours still fresh.
HORSTEINER ABTSBERG-REUCHSBERG Riesling
(Long ago, when Hampstead and Highgate entertained, that was the dinner-party wine to drink.)

In Rome the sun shines, and I take heart.

Every day, it seems, the newspapers have another story about a break-through in cancer research. In laboratories genes are isolated; soon there will be the technology to zap them and to cultivate replacements. For trial patients meanwhile conditions can be steadied, the disease may go into a clean remission.

Every day there are fresh examples of human ingenuity and wilfulness beating the medical odds.

I live on still, always in hope.

The book proceeds.

Xeroxes of my ballpoint copy of The Lantern Bearers were posted off yesterday. The score has gone from me, literally; but I shall endure a little in it, for as long as Bone's fame lasts.

The pages of my original, torn out of a school jotter, are speckled with rust-coloured damp spots. They still reek of the thirty-odd years they were left secreted beneath the bungalow's floorboards.

I've emerged from my long darkness too. It may be only a short-term reprieve, who knows. There has been just enough time to date: time for me to give the music back, and to exult and sing out Bone's song.